SOLD

DENA MCDONALD

Printed in the United States of America
First Printing 2021
First Edition 2021

ISBN: 978-1-7369533-0-3

10 9 8 7 6 5 4 3 2 1

Cover Design by: Pro-ebookcovers
Editing by: Jessie Raymond

Thank you to my family whom I love dearly:

My Husband Tim

My Son Alex and my Granddaughter Sofia

My Son Josh and my Daughter-in-law Jane

My Mother Sara

My Mother-in-law Carol

A special thank you to my supporters:

Gary, Sandy, Erik and Brian Cooper

Erica File

CHAPTER 1

"Maria, it's Javier, can you hear me? Wake up my love!" Javier's face lit up with excitement as he fell down to one knee, hovering over the side of the bed. I started to slowly open my eyes, trying to focus but my vision was a little blurry. His voice penetrating my ears, I cautiously moved my head to look in his direction. I moved my arms a bit, then my legs, feeling the aches in my body.

"I can't believe it. My beautiful wife has come back to me!" His eyes expressing happiness as he leaned over to kiss me on the cheek, then my forehead. Leaning into my body as close as he could get, trying to give me a hug.

Suddenly the bedroom door opened. A plump lady with a round face, and salt and pepper hair rolled up into a bun on the top of her head shouted.

"What is wrong Mr. Alatorre?!"

"Maria's waking up. Esmeralda, call Dr. Ruiz." She wasted no time. She grabbed the handset of the telephone on the table next to me and summoned the doctor.

As I was lying in bed I could hear the conversation going on but I couldn't talk or react. I felt weak. After a minute or two I managed to move my head, looking around but not recognizing the room. It was unfamiliar to me. I was in this very luxurious room. The bed was soft and welcoming, the wall of windows on my left let the sunshine in just enough to feel the warmth. Beautiful paintings hung on most of the walls. Yet I was very unsure.

"Dr. Ruiz is on his way Mr. Alatorre," Esmeralda said as she hung up the phone. She reached for my hand, rubbing it with love and kindness.

"I will go get you some water in the meantime," as she turned away I quietly whispered, "Thank you."

"Maria? How do you feel?" The man asked.

"Who are you?"

"I'm your husband, Javier," he said in a gentle voice. "That was Esmeralda our housekeeper."

"My husband?" I asked softly.

"Do you not remember anything? The accident?"

"No." I started to tear up, feeling scared.

"Don't worry Dr. Ruiz is on his way," he took one of my hands and started to rub it gently, trying to calm me down.

He explained to me that I was in a coma for about a month caused by a car accident. Dr. Ruiz and Esmeralda have been taking care of me.

Within no time Dr. Ruiz showed up, examined me and asked me some questions. I watched Dr. Ruiz's facial expressions hoping to get a sense of what he was thinking.

He is an old man with crazy, wild black hair, short stature and round spectacles too big for his face. His mouth moved with great proclamation. His face showed his age and wisdom. His arms animated as if they were trying to talk by themselves.

Stepping away from the bed, he talked to Javier privately. Dr. Ruiz handed him a bottle of medication, pointing at the bottle and then glancing at me every so often.

Turning his attention to me, he said, "Maria, I believe you are experiencing a case of Amnesia from the car accident. When you were in a coma we performed two tests called an MRI and a CT Scan that also indicated this. It may take a while for you to recover so be patient; in the meantime, I am going to give you some medicine that may help."

I looked at Javier. I could see that he was trying to be strong for me, trying not to get emotional. I however did not react at all. I felt empty. *Is this real?*

"When you feel better I will need you to come to my office and have more tests done," he said as he turned towards Javier again.

Dr. Ruiz pulled Javier to the side once more, closer to the wall of windows and started talking. I could hear bits and pieces of their conversation but to be honest I didn't care. I was struggling with my own emotions.

"Mr. Alatorre, make sure you give her one to two pills a day. Make sure you keep track, it's very important. I need to know what dosage is working."

"I understand. Let me walk you to the door Dr. Ruiz." As they walked out of the room, Esmeralda came in, gave me a glass of water, a small amount of food and made sure I was comfortable.

"I know that this has been hard for you Mrs. Alatorre but you don't have to worry. I am going to take good care of you."

"Is this my home?" I asked.

"You and Mr. Alatorre have lived here for a long time."

"How long have we been married?"

"Over Twenty-Five years I believe." She said as she began straightening out the bed covers.

"Did anyone else get hurt in the accident?" I was worried that maybe I had caused it.

"No."

I sighed in relief.

"The most important thing right now is that you are here with us. You need to focus on your recovery."

I watched her walk over to the bedroom door and press a button on a digital keypad. Window shades started to lower over the wall of windows, blocking the setting sun from penetrating the bedroom any further.

"I am going to spend the night here just in case you need me. Try to get some rest." She picked up my empty plate. "I will be back soon to check on you." She walked out of the room, closing the door behind her.

I spent the rest of the evening in bed resting, trying to remember the accident, trying to remember anything. My head started hurting from all the stress so I closed my eyes and slowly drifted off to sleep. Throughout the night I could hear cracking noises from the door opening and closing. I knew Javier or Esmeralda were probably checking on me but I never raised my head in response. I just laid there, wondering why I couldn't even remember my own husband, Esmeralda, or anyone for that matter.

The next morning, I woke up feeling better. I rolled over from my side and onto my back and looked around to see if I was alone. Nobody was in the room so I sat up in bed. I thought for sure that I would feel pain or at least be sore but I felt nothing. I felt good!

Resting against a pile of soft pillows, I scanned the room waiting a bit to see if someone would come in. Nobody showed up so after a few minutes so I decided to get out of bed and try walking around. I initially felt a little dizzy so I sat on the edge of the bed for a moment until my head cleared. Standing up, I headed towards a door that was slightly ajar. I pushed the door gently. It opened to showcase a very spacious and beautiful bathroom fashioned with the finest finishes. An expansive mirror hung over a granite counter top with two sink bowls. Walking over to it, I looked at myself, not recognizing the woman standing before me. I leaned in a little closer, looking at myself, touching my face. I noticed that my long black hair paired perfectly with my olive skin. I have green eyes, full lips and perfectly manicured eyebrows.

Satisfied with what I saw I returned to exploring this magnificent room.

Attached to the bathroom was a closet full of clothes, shoes, purses; everything a girl desired. In the center of the closet was a large, square dresser, waist high full of drawers. And on the other side of the closet, I could see men's clothes; Javier's clothes.

As I was walking around, taking in everything around me, hoping that by seeing all this, it would trigger a memory but it didn't. Nothing, nothing at all. I stood in the same place feeling a sense of despair, trying to hold back the tears building up in my eyes when all of the sudden I could hear a female voice calling out.

"Mrs. Alatorre are you ok?" It was Esmeralda. I walked out of the bathroom to meet her. She was standing in the middle of the room with a big smile on her face. She walked over to me, putting her arms out to indicate she wanted a hug. I welcomed her embrace. It felt good.

"I see you're feeling better."

I nodded at her with a smile.

"Mr. Alatorre had to go out for business this morning. If you're feeling up to it we can go to the kitchen and I will make you something to eat. You need to take your medicine too. Do you feel like eating?"

"Sure, that sounds lovely."

Esmeralda led the way. We walked down a hallway full of paintings and sculptures. It was beautiful. The hallway eventually opened up into a large living room that was two stories high, a wall of windows to the left displaying an ice blue ocean just steps away. I thought, *this is where I live? Am I this lucky in my life to have a loving husband and a home that could only be described as magnificent?*

"Here we are Mrs. Alatorre. Have a seat somewhere and rest while I make you something special." She walked towards the sink, made a glass of water, walked backed to me while grabbing a bottle of medicine out of her apron pocket.

"Here you go. Take these two pills."

"Thank you, do you know what happened? In the accident I mean."

"Mr. Alatorre doesn't like to talk about it but I was told that someone drove into your lane, you swerved to avoid them and crashed into a ravine. Luckily there was a witness who called an ambulance."

"I'm glad nobody else got hurt." I took another sip from my glass of water.

"It's so beautiful here." I said as I looked outside at the ocean. "Where are we?"

"Mazatlán." She walked over to a desk in the kitchen, opened a drawer and took out a book of maps. Flipping through the pages, she finally found what she was looking for. "In Mexico." She stated as she pointed, showing me the page.

I flashed Esmeralda a thank you smile before she turned to put the book back in its place, then walking to the stove to make our food.

We had a wonderful day together. Esmeralda showed me what a typical day was like for her. I followed her around like a child learning for the first time. She explained to me that Javier usually works long hours and that I spend my days either helping Javier at work, shopping or hanging around the house.

Javier ended up coming home late that evening. I was on the veranda, sitting on an outdoor couch, taking in the scenery, resting and wondering. Javier sat down next to me, put his arm around one of my shoulders, crossed one leg over the other and leaned in towards me.

"I am sorry that I was not here when you woke up this morning. I had something important to deal with that couldn't wait."

"It's fine. Esmeralda helped me a lot today."

"How are you feeling my delicate flower?"

"I thought I would be sore when I tried to get out of bed this morning, but I'm good." I tried to wiggle away from him a bit. He felt like a stranger to me.

He leaned over, kissed me on my cheek and said, "Next weekend is our Anniversary. I know this is hard for you and I understand if you feel like you're not ready but I would like to have a small party with our family and friends. Kind of an Anniversary and 'we love you' party. What do you think?"

Anniversary? Meeting people I don't know. I don't remember. All the questions, all the unrecognizable faces!

"It won't be a lot of people" he said.

He must have seen the expression on my face as I was processing my thoughts.

"Just a small get together? You promise?" I asked.

"Yes, I promise."

CHAPTER 2

The following week flew by. Every day, Esmeralda took time out of her work day to spend with me. She showed me photographs, especially of the people who are going to attend our Anniversary party. She told me stories about my life. It made me feel more and more comfortable with myself, Javier and the life we have.

Finally it was party night. I felt so nervous! I couldn't even decide on what outfit to wear. The blue one, the red one, the one with sparkles? So many choices! So many thoughts were flying in my head, and at the forefront was the question; "Why do I feel so much pressure to impress people I don't remember?" Then I went, "I am overthinking this. I'm just going to wear what feels like me."

Me! Do I even know me?

I closed my eyes for a second, took a deep breath and grabbed the first outfit that I was drawn to. It was a cute, all white jumpsuit with a soft, flowy pant. I took it off the hanger and said to myself, "*This feels like me.*"

As I finished getting ready for our party, I found myself shaking a bit, trembling inside. I tried telling myself everything would be fine as I looked in the mirror one more time and headed towards the party.

Walking down the hallway, I started to hear muttered voices coming from behind a door that always seemed to be shut; Javier's home office. I cautiously walked up to the door, pressed my ear against it. Two men were talking, one sounded like Javier. I could only hear what they were saying in bits.

"…can't remember…" a deep voice stated.

"…it's working…" Javier said.

"Is the doctor confident?" A woman entered the conversation.

"He seems to be." All of the sudden I heard the shuffling of footsteps, they were getting louder, they're coming towards the door! I started walking, trying to be as quiet as possible. I could hear the door opening as I walked farther down the hall. I turned my head around to see what was happening. Javier, a man and a woman came out. I tried to keep my composure hoping they would not suspect that I was trying to listen to their conversation.

"Maria! It's me Ava, Ava Valdez."

She walked towards me, reaching out, grabbing both of my hands, standing directly in front of me like a mirror.

"How are you feeling? We are all so happy to see you."

I stood silent, not recognizing her face at all. I looked at Javier briefly then said, "I'm doing well, thank you."

Javier butted in, "Maria, Ava is one of your friends. She also works for me." Javier then put his hand on top of Mateo's shoulder. "This is Mateo, Ava's husband and one of my top employees."

"We were all so worried. Come, come with me." She let go of one of my hands, kept a hold of the other one as we walked together outside onto the veranda where there was a small group of people. Most of them noticed us right away. Some were looking at us with smiles on their faces and some were whispering to each other. As we stopped walking, I glanced around at all the faces but could not recognize any. Feeling anxious inside, I lowered my head down a bit to look at the ground, feeling all of these strangers' eyes upon me was overwhelming. Javier walked up behind me, put a hand on the middle of my back and announced to the group.

"Everybody, let us welcome our Maria back. Show her patience, love and share your stories so that one day she may remember her life."

Javier then turned to me and whispered in my ear, "Don't worry, I will stay by your side tonight."

I just nodded at him with a smile. I kind of looked around again, waiting to see what would happen. I notice Ava had walked away and started a conversation with other people. Javier continued his conversation with the same man from his office.

After a few minutes I tapped Javier on his arm and asked, "Where is my family?"

Javier turned to face me, giving me his full attention and told me, "I'm sorry but there is no one from your family that is here tonight."

"Why not?"

"Most of them have passed away or live too far away. You really don't have any contact with them."

"I'm all alone?"

"No, you have me. We take care of each other." He leaned in to give me a small peck on the cheek.

As I met more and more people, I felt at ease. It turned out to be a wonderful night. The veranda was decorated with accent lights throughout. The soft glow was relaxing and romantic. There was a food buffet and a wait staff providing drinks. You could hear everyone talking to each other while the ocean waves crashed in the background. The fresh, warm, salty air was intoxicating, creating a relaxed mood for everyone. As the night went on, I heard stories about me, family, friends and vacations that Javier and I took. Nothing sounding familiar though, nothing triggering any memories but everyone was so nice that I felt at home for the first time.

CHAPTER 3

After a couple of weeks I felt more and more comfortable around the house. Some days I spend my time following Esmeralda and bombarding her with questions or helping her clean. I enjoy hanging out with Esmeralda. She is not only my housekeeper, but my friend whom I have come to love.

My evenings were spent with Javier, listening to his stories about how we met, our wedding, our life together and asking questions that he answers with such gusto that it makes me giggle sometimes. One evening, we stayed up so late that we could barely get out of bed the next morning for my first doctor's appointment.

"Knock, knock, knock," Esmeralda was knocking softly at the bedroom door. Javier raised his head off the pillow and said quietly, "What is it?"

"It's getting late Sir. I just wanted to make sure you two were awake."

Javier quickly glanced at the clock on the table next to him, then rolled over on his back to see if I was still sleeping.

"We're up. We will be down soon."

"Ok Sir." I could hear her walking away.

As I laid on my side of the bed, Javier continued to roll over in my direction, getting closer to me. He reached over and touched me without saying anything, softly caressing my cheek, staring intensely into my eyes.

I could feel his passion for me. For the most part, I felt at ease but there was still a part of me that was holding back, uncomfortable and unsure.

I reached out to touch him on the arm that was caressing me and said, "Good morning."

"How are you feeling about today's visit?" He asked.

"Hoping to hear good news."

"Think positive thoughts." He kissed me on my forehead, got out of bed and got dressed. I followed behind him getting ready myself. We both went to the kitchen to eat breakfast.

Esmeralda is a wonderful cook. To my surprise she set a table for us on the veranda. The sky was overcast but it was still refreshing. Esmeralda brought us our food, drinks but no medicine. I couldn't take it before my test. We enjoyed our time together, eating and talking, but time was going by quickly.

Javier looked at his watch and said, "We need to leave Maria."

We both grabbed a few things, then made our way to the car and drove to Dr. Ruiz's office in the city.

When we arrived I noticed that the office was empty. *Where is his staff?* I thought to myself.

"Hello!" Dr. Ruiz said as he welcomed us to his office.

"Hello." Javier said in response. The two men reaching out to shake hands.

"How have you been feeling Mrs. Alatorre?"

"Pretty good." I said without thinking.

"That's good to hear. No reaction to the medication I gave you? No side effects?" He asked while looking at me first, then glancing at Javier for a reaction.

"None that I can think of." I answered as I turned my head towards Javier. He smiled at me to show that he was in agreement.

"Wonderful! Today we are going to do an MRI. This will let me see if anything has changed from your last one and hopefully see some improvements." He gestured for us to follow him.

When we entered the testing room he first told me to change into a gown. Then I was told to lay down on the table. Dr. Ruiz then pressed a button which caused the table to slide into the machine so that he could run the scan. I laid quietly listening to the machine make humming noises while Dr. Ruiz and Javier were in another room watching through a glass window.

"Is she still taking the medicine properly?" Dr. Ruiz asked Javier.

"Esmeralda is with her most of the day and she hasn't said anything to me. So I am assuming that she is."

"I am not seeing any changes in her scan. I am going to keep her on the same dosage for now."

When the testing was done Dr. Ruiz escorted us to the front door, telling us that he would call after he looked at the scan results closer. He told us not to worry and that from what he saw so far everything looked good.

On our way home Javier asked if I wanted to take a boat ride. The testing didn't take as long as he thought it would and he doesn't have a lot to do at work, so he wanted to spend the rest of the day pampering me. How could I refuse!

When we got home we took the boat out for a couple of hours and even invited Esmeralda along for the ride. She was very happy to get out of the house and into the fresh air. It was so enjoyable. Javier drove the boat while Esmeralda and I gossiped like we were lifelong best friends.

CHAPTER 4

The next morning a few of my men picked me up for work. After getting into the car, we drove down the road, eventually heading north along the city's main road leading into the countryside. Eventually we pulled into an empty parking lot that was off the side of the road. A few of my other me were waiting for us in a black SUV and a cargo van. We were heading to a meeting to buy more girls. The demand has been up lately and I'm not complaining.

After traveling a few minutes, we made our way onto a gravel road nestled along the ocean. I looked out the tinted window next to me and noticed that it had started to rain. The wind was blowing through the small trees scattered along the shoreline. I became mesmerized by the chaotic nature of the waves crashing against the rocky shore.

My two men in the front seats were having a conversation between themselves while I sat in silence; enjoying the peace for once. After about twenty minutes, one of them said, "We're here Boss."

The SUV that was in front pulled up next to a rundown warehouse with large, rusty garage doors. One of my men jumped out to open one of the garage doors so that my SUV and the cargo van could pull inside. Driving inside, we slowly passed several men waiting, armed with guns and an attitude. The rest of my men walked in on foot, fully armed. Both cars finally came to a stop.

My driver picked up a gun that was sitting on his lap while the other man in the front passenger seat grabbed a black duffle bag that was lodged between his feet on the floor. After they both stepped out of the car, they signaled to me that it was safe to exit.

"Welcome Mr. Alatorre. We have some good choices for you today," said an older man with white hair and a handlebar mustache to match.

"Better than the last time I hope."

"Yes, younger and prettier I would say."

The old man gestured for everyone to follow him. I walked side by side with him, with some of my other men following and a few staying by the cars.

The warehouse was a giant open space with junk laying around as if it was the local trash dump. We walked to the other side of the building towards a door that was rotten and hanging half off its hinges. The old man opened the damaged door so we could enter. I immediately noticed that it looked like a hospitable room; beds with disheveled sheets, old equipment covered in dust. Still walking from room to room we eventually made our way into a darker room with low lighting. This dimly lit room had a couple of more men sitting around, talking and smoking but when the old man and myself entered, they stood up out of respect.

"Open the door," said the old man gesturing towards it.

A younger man with a missing eye covered by a patch walked to a black door with paint chipping off of it, unlocked the door and opened it. The old man walked in and turned on a light, I followed.

"So what do you think?" pointing toward the girls.

I took a look around. The girls were squirming, holding each other, trying to comfort each other, hoping they wouldn't be chosen. I took a closer look at a few of them.

One in particular grabbed my attention. Walking up to her, I reached for her face, grabbing her chin and turning her head from side to side to get a good look. I didn't say anything, then moved on to the next one.

I turned away from the girls and said, "Good job. I am happy, very happy." I gestured for the duffle bag. One of my guy's with tattoos covering his neck and arms dropped the bag next to the old man's feet. I pointed to the five girls that I wanted. The young man with the eye patch walked over to them, told them to put their hands behind their backs and put zip ties around their wrists. The other remaining girls started screaming at the men to let them go but they knew they had no real power. The five chosen girls were escorted to the cargo van without incident while everyone else followed behind, talking amongst themselves. When we got back to the cars, I turned to the white haired man and said, "Keep this up and we will be doing business for a long time." With both hands in the pockets of his oversized jeans, the old man simply smiled and nodded.

All the girls were loaded up, my men safely back into their cars. We drove away one by one. The SUV that was parked outside went first, then the cargo van and then mine. We drove in a uniform line, the rain starting to subside.

It was about fifteen minutes until we came upon a small cargo dock yard. Slowly driving through the property, watching carefully for anything out of the ordinary, each man was cautiously looking around with guns in hand.

In the distance, a cargo boat that was docked began to appear. As we got closer, I could see shipping containers being hoisted from the ground onto the boat. Men walking around, working fast. One of these men started waving at our line of cars approaching, then pointing for us to drive to the left. He started jogging so he could meet my men and I at an open container. When the cars stopped, I jumped out to greet the man. My men exited their SUVs too, some walking to assist me, and the others getting the girls out of the back of the van.

"Load them up in this one!" The man, maybe in his mid-thirties, yelled while pointing to the open shipping container. He was strutting around at first, checking things out, and walked up to me afterwards to shake my hand.

"How are things? Everything on track?" I inquired.

"Yes, we are good to go. My contacts are on route. We will have this done in no time." The man reached into his pocket to grab a cigarette and lighter. While listening to me talk, he lit his cigarette and started smoking.

"These girls are top of the line so I expect them to get there safely."

"Hey! No worries!" He stopped to take a puff. "The container is set up for the ride. They're in good hands."

"They better be." I started to walk closer to the containers to make sure things were going smoothly and looked inside, making sure it was good enough for transporting. The girls were squirming, making noise, knowing their fate. Their eyes tearing up with desperation and despair.

I told one of my men. "Make sure they are branded before shipping. I want their buyers to know who to come to when they want the best girls."

My men started cutting their hands free, telling them to sit down and be quiet, and then began branding each one with my mark under their belly button.

The container was packed with supplies; bottled water, blankets and food. After the last girl was branded, my men walked out, closing the doors one by one, with the girls' faces slowly disappearing into the darkness.

CHAPTER 5

"DREAMING"

It's been a couple of months now. I have settled into my life with Javier. I feel like I have a daily routine, a purpose to my life. Both my body and mind feel good, other than having to take medicine for my headaches. I tell myself to be positive, to keep moving forward and that is what I am doing.

I was strolling through the house when a photograph in a colorful picture frame caught my eye. It was Javier and me on a yacht. We looked so happy in the picture. The water was clear blue, the sun was setting in the background and we were in matching white clothes, clinging two glasses of wine. *I have an idea! I'm going to ask Javier if we can take the boat out and do an overnight trip.*

When Javier got home from work, Esmeralda and I were in the kitchen making dinner. We had music playing while we cooked, singing loudly and making some dance moves in between.

"Hello ladies! I see we're having fun tonight." Javier said as he sniffed in the aroma. "The food smells wonderful!"

"Javie! Yes, Esmeralda is teaching me some tricks." I walked over to welcome him home. He grabbed me around my waist, with a smile on his face, he dipped me and gave me a wildly passionate kiss.

"Wow! That was nice." I said.

"Well, I like it when you call me Javie and seeing you happy makes me happy."

"Ok Mr. and Mrs. Alatorre dinner is ready. Would you like to sit inside or outside?"

"Outside!" We said in unison. Javier grabbed my hand and escorted me outside. We walked to the table, Javier pulled a chair out for me while asking me what I did today.

"I'm glad you asked. I saw a photo today of us on our yacht. I was hoping we could go on an overnight trip together."

Javier sat down, put a napkin on his lap, took a sip of the wine that Esmeralda just put on the table and said, "I like that idea. How about this weekend? We can go to Isla de Venados."

"Oh I am so excited! I can't wait. Just you and me on an adventure."

He picked up his glass of wine, directed it out towards me. I picked up my glass and we clinked them together while smiling at each other. We finished eating our meal while talking about our trip.

We had a few days before our excursion so while Javier worked, Esmeralda and I started figuring out what we needed. We made a list and started packing the things we could do without until the day of our trip.

The next day, Ava came over to take me shopping. We walked around glancing in all the store windows, deciding what I needed, what I wanted and what I desired. Becoming tired and hungry, we stopped at this cute cafe with an outside seating area that overlooked a rocky shore. It was so pretty. There were green vines hanging from wood beams, light strands hung over the entire patio area and waves crashing dangerously close to the concrete patio.

After we ordered our drinks and food, Ava told me a story or two about other boat trips we had taken with

Mateo and herself. She told me how fun it is to be on the water, being away from the city and just relaxing. The more we talked, the more excited I became.

After a whirlwind day of shopping, eating and gossiping, Ava dropped me off at home a little bit before Javier got there, just in time for dinner.

That evening, after dinner, Javier and I brought a few of our packed things out to the yacht. We didn't want to do it all on the day we left. As we finished up on the boat, Javier's phone started ringing. It is always ringing. Telling me he needed to take the call, I went ahead and walked up to the house by myself, giving him a good bye wave.

"Hello?" He said.

He stood still for a minute or two listening to the voice on the phone. Then replied, "You need to take care of this matter. I am not cancelling my trip with Maria." He hung up the phone and headed to the house, mumbling words under his breath as he walked.

The morning came very fast. I thought to myself....*I sure am glad I started preparing for the trip when I did!* Javier wasn't in the bedroom so I figured he was already eating breakfast or at the boat. I couldn't help but smile while briskly walking to the kitchen, dragging my suitcase behind me. Javier was in the kitchen with Esmeralda having a conversation.

"Good morning Mrs. Alatorre. Your breakfast is ready," pointing to the table.

"Are you ready for our trip?" Javier inquired knowing the answer.

"Yes, I can't wait to leave."

"The boat is packed and ready to go. We can take off as soon as you are ready."

I sat down to eat, thanking them both for doing everything they did this morning. I finished my breakfast with excitement and gusto, jumped up and told Javie that I was ready. I walked over to where my luggage was, grabbed it and headed out the door.

"Come on Javie! Let's start our adventure!"

"Ok. Ok." He giggled a little. "We're off Esmeralda. See you Sunday afternoon."

Javier jogged to catch up to me. He took my suitcase from my hand, switched it to the other side and said, "My delicate flower doesn't carry luggage."

I looked at him smiling, took his hand and leaned into his body to give him as close to a hug as I could get. We got on the boat, got everything settled and then headed out. It was a warm day already. The sun was shining with just a few clouds in the sky. While Javie drove the boat, I made some drinks for us. He clearly knew what he was doing. Handling the wind and waves like an expert. I stood by his side watching, trying to learn, and thinking perhaps he will let me have a try at driving when we are farther out.

Isla de Venados, also known as Deer Island, is only a few miles away from our dock. Since it is a quick ride, we can spend most of our day having fun.

As we got closer to the island, I noticed more and more boats. Some large, some small. I was a little disappointed because I was hoping for more privacy but we can just keep our distance. Javier must have noticed the expression on my face because he said, "We are going to go around to the other side where it is more private. This side has a lot of the sand beaches but the other side is more rugged and romantic."

We sailed our way around to the other side, dodging boats, kayaks and wave runners. We came upon an area where the water was light blue, and shallow, maybe fifteen to twenty feet deep. Javier stopped the boat and dropped the anchor. I looked over the side, fish of all colors and sizes were gathering around the boat, checking us out. Being here felt natural, like this is where I belonged. This is something I must have enjoyed doing in the past. I turned to Javier.

"Let's go swimming!"

I ran to the bedroom, opened my suitcase and picked out a swimming suit. As I was getting ready, it dawned on me that I forgot to take my medicine again. I wouldn't worry but this is three days in a row now. I desperately looked through my toiletry bag, nothing. I looked in every pocket in every bag, nothing. I came to realize that I must have left it at the house.

I felt terrible. I thought to myself, we just got here. I can't tell him. It will be ok. I feel fine. I don't want to ruin this.

Javier walked in. "I thought you were getting dressed?"

"Oh, yes. It just took me awhile to decide on which swimsuit to wear. I'll get us some towels and wait for you on the back deck." I reached over to touch him on his arm so I could make him feel at ease and not draw more attention to the situation.

"All right. I'll see you in a minute."

After finding some towels, I walked out onto the lowest deck in the back of the boat that just grazed the water's edge. I sat down at the end, put my feet into the water, swirling them around and around, looking into the blue wondering if the fish were watching me. I started to get lost in my own daydreaming then I heard a loud thump! Javier practically jumped over my head into the water making a huge splash! I pulled my legs out of the water, up towards my chest in reaction. After I realized what had happened, I too jumped into the water, trying to land as close to him as I could.

We played in the water the entire day; swimming, snorkeling, laying on floating rafts with drinks in our hands. The day just flew by.

The sun started getting low in the sky, we became so hungry that we scrambled to make dinner as fast as we could. Each of us doing our part; cooking, putting plates and silverware out, and mixing drinks. We were completely in sync with each other. Finally we were ready to eat! We sat outside at a deck table under the clear evening skies with a warm breeze on our skin and sea birds chirping all around us.

We were just getting ready to eat when Javier said, "Oh I almost forgot." He walked briskly into the cabin, flipped on a switch and voila! The entire boat lit up with string lights. When he got back to the table I reached my hand out in search of his.

"Oh my goodness! It's beautiful!"

"We certainly can't have a romantic dinner without the perfect ambiance. Besides, it will make my cooking taste so much better," he jokingly said with a smile.

We finished eating our meal and spent the rest of our evening embracing the privacy and the quiet. Javier told me stories about other vacations we took and at one point we turned on some music and did a little slow dancing, drank some wine, anything we could think of to make the night special. Eventually we made our way to the bedroom where we made love for the first time and eventually fell asleep…

"What are you doing!" I said.

"I'm sorry! I'm sorry! I don't know what else to do!"

"Why? I don't understand Josh!"

I looked around in a daze, feeling confused and desperate. My legs starting to feel weak. Unable to hold my body up anymore, I fell into a chair next to me. Opening my eyes, closing my eyes, feeling the heaviness of them while trying to watch what was taking place. A scruffy-looking man handed a duffle bag to my husband. Two other men, who were also standing on the boat deck, dropped four more bags next to his feet.

My husband asked the men to give him a minute to say goodbye to me.

I woke up, rolling around in bed, breathing heavily, full of anxiety, thinking to myself...*that dream was too real.* I rolled over to see if Javie was still in bed but he was already up. I wasn't feeling very well. Too much to drink maybe?

I decided to take a quick shower. The hot water and steam felt good against my skin. My head feeling queasy, I stood motionless for a bit letting the confined shower stall fill up with steam. A tap on the glass door startled me. I turned around to see Javie standing outside with some food in his hand. He opened the door to slip me a piece of fruit but I brushed it away.

"I don't feel like eating just yet."

"Not feeling good?"

"Just a little too much to drink I think. It'll pass."

"When you get out, take your medicine. That may help." Of course I just agreed with him.

"I'm not going to admit I left it at home. I'll play this out and see how I feel in a bit," I thought to myself. I stepped out of the shower, got dressed and went up to meet Javie. He wasn't where I expected him to be so I walked to the front of the boat where I saw him standing, facing the water, talking on his phone. He seemed upset, so I held up a bit and stood there waiting until he was done. I leaned against the side of the boat while holding onto the railing on the other side to steady myself. Bobbing up and down with the water didn't exactly make me feel better.

"Mateo, I need you and Ava to schedule another shipment for me. Just as good as the last one, same offer."

He went silent for a moment listening to Mateo.

"Ok, call me with the time and place." He hung up his phone and placed it in shirt pocket. I waited for a few seconds and then approached him, trying to make it appear as if I was feeling better. I did not want to ruin the only time we had left.

"So what is the plan for today?" I grabbed him around the waist to give him a morning hug.

"Whatever you want," he said while snuggling up against me.

"Maybe we could go ashore and explore a bit." I said.

"I'm in. How about taking a wave runner? You can hop on the back. I'll teach you how to drive and then we can switch on the way back."

"Sounds like fun!" However, all I could think about was the bobbing up and down.

We only had a few hours until we had to leave but we made the best out of it; it was fun. All the exploring put me in a better mood and made me forget about how I was feeling. Before we got ready to head back home, we made a quick lunch, and packed some things away. Javie pulled up the anchor and while he drove us back, I enjoyed the scenery.

When we got home, Esmeralda met us at the dock to help bring all the cargo back to the house. It was exhausting but we got it all done before dark. She even helped me carry my suitcase and other items to my bedroom. Quietly I asked her if she would help me look for my medicine.

"You forgot to take your medicine Mrs. Alatorre?"

"No. I actually forgot it. I couldn't believe it." I said, disgusted with myself. "Please don't tell Javie."

"Let me see if I can find it." Esmeralda looked through a few dresser drawers, then in the bathroom, then left the room saying, "I'm going to check the kitchen."

"Thank you."

Esmeralda walked down the hall, about halfway she glanced back at our bedroom, then entered Javier's office. He was sitting at his wooden desk. An antique desk that was carved with exquisite details on the front and sides.

Looking at his computer, the light from the screen was shining in his face as his eyes moved back and forth reading.

He heard Esmeralda walk in, "What can I do for you Esmeralda?"

As she walked up to him, she put a finger over the center of her mouth indicating for him to be quieter. She walked closer to his desk and whispered, "Did you know Mrs. Alatorre did not take her pills the other day?"

"No. She did wake up not feeling good but she blamed the wine."

"Should we call Dr. Ruiz?"

He hesitated for a moment. "Is she acting normal?"

"She seems the same to me. I'm helping her find them now."

"Keep looking. Let me know. I may call the doctor tomorrow."

Esmeralda nodded her head in agreement and left the room. Javier sat at his desk for a moment thinking about what to do. He had other important matters to worry about at that moment so he continued reading on his computer.

Esmeralda looked in the kitchen even though she had not seen the bottle of medicine there the whole weekend. She looked outside on the patio area just in case it was dropped, but nothing. She looked in the grass and on the walkway to the boat dock, still nothing. She decided to head back into the house, glancing around as she walked and for some reason, she looked towards the picture frame of Javie and me on the living room shelf. There it was, the bottle was sitting next to the frame. The one I had looked at the other day. Esmeralda grabbed it and headed back to the bedroom.

"Here you go Mrs. Alatorre. I found them!"

"Where were they?"

"On the shelf, by the yacht picture."

She reached out to hand them to me, I took them from her and said, "I totally forgot that I stopped at the picture before we left. I must have put them down."

"Well, you have them now. I'll go get a glass of water for you."

"That's ok," I said. "I will just take them now in the bathroom."

"I'm gonna go home then. Goodnight."

"Goodnight."

On her way out, Esmeralda walked back into Javier's office to let him know that she found my medicine. She also informed him that I had taken them and that she was heading home.

CHAPTER 6

Getting home is not easy for Esmeralda, she has to make three bus transfers just to get into her neighborhood. The second bus ride is when she travels from the luxurious lifestyle of the wealthy to the reality of the lower class.

About thirty minutes later, she finally stepped off the bus. A block down the street from her home. She lived in a yellow house with wrought iron bars over the windows, a front door with peeling paint and a front porch that shows its age.

As Esmeralda walked up to her house, she noticed all the lights were on inside. Curious as to why? Her only daughter Lucy is usually at work. She unlocked the front door, pushed it open to find her daughter sitting on the couch, being over shadowed by a man standing in front of her.

"Lucy? Who is this?" Esmeralda inquired.

The man turned around, put the hat from his hoodie over his head and walked silently by Esmeralda out the door.

"He's just a friend." Lucy said annoyed.

"Why are you not at work?"

Lucy popped off the couch with a grimace look on her face, feeling annoyed by her mother butting in her life.

"Someone at work asked me to switch nights." She said as she walked away, down the hall and into her bedroom.

Esmeralda was surprised at the exchange as usually, Lucy and her get along very well. However, she was too tired to talk about it now. She needed to get some sleep and couldn't take the chance of being up all night talking; at least not tonight. The next day was still another work day like always.

Lucy was still in bed the next morning so Esmeralda decided to leave her a quick note, knowing that it was Lucy's turn to have the night off the day after.

Let's talk tonight when I get home. Love Mom.

Esmeralda started her day at work in the kitchen making breakfast. Javier had already left for work and I was getting dressed, taking my medicine; basically, my morning routine. As I walked to the kitchen I could smell the food.

"Good morning Esmeralda. How are you today?"

"I am tired. Got into it a little with my daughter last night."

"You have a daughter? How did I not know this yet?"

"Sorry Mrs. Alatorre. Her name is Lucy. Sometimes I forget about your amnesia."

"I understand. Is everything okay between you two?"

"Yes, it will be." She said while walking my plate of food over to the table. "Taken your medicine yet?"

"Yes ma'am."

We chatted for a bit while I ate, our conversation ending naturally. After Esmeralda was done in the kitchen, she moved onto another part of the house.

Today was an unusual day for me. I really didn't know what to do with myself. Life is back to normal for

Javier. He goes to work everyday now. Esmeralda's not by my side helping me anymore, being subjected to my never-ending questions. It can be a bit frustrating, feeling like I have no purpose. I decided to keep exploring the house so I went downstairs for the first time. I never had a reason to go down there so this was an excellent time to find out what I was missing.

I headed down the steps to find a bar area, pool table, poker table and a big screen TV. Nothing here for a girl to see. I kept walking. There are a couple of bedrooms, a storage room and then I came upon the most intriguing room. It was a large room with stone walls except for two. One was a wall stocked with wine bottles behind huge glass doors and the other was a wall of books. There were a few tables and leather chairs scattered throughout. The lighting was more subdued than the other rooms so it was a little hard to see every detail. I noticed how chilly it was compared to the other rooms, probably because of the wine, but the cold feel gave it a cave-like atmosphere. As I finished scanning the room, I decided to walk over to the bookcase.

Look at all these books, I thought.

I was very excited so I started reading the titles to see if anything caught my eye. I needed something to do so I thought to myself, "Why not read a book?" I searched and searched until I saw a bright red book. It was sticking out a little farther than the others so I thought, *this must have been read recently.*

I reached for it with excitement, pulled it out and started to open it. Whoa! Did the bookcase just shake?

I looked up, down, left, right. It looked odd so I stepped back to get an overall view and noticed that the right side was pushed away from the wall. I walked over to it, put the book back in its place, reached behind the shelf and pulled it outward. It was a secret room. I wasn't sure what I wanted to do. I looked back towards the front of the room to see if anyone was around. There was nobody in sight so I decided to venture in.

The dark hallway had a smell of moisture in the air, and the lights on the walls were placed about every thirty to thirty-five feet. Just enough to get down the hallway and illuminate small rooms that looked like jail cells. I walked slowly down the hall, looking cautiously in every room. All of them dark and empty, smelling of mold. I must have walked a hundred yards before I noticed that the hallway was getting a little brighter. An exit ahead maybe? As I walked by one room, I noticed something dangling from the door. I stopped to touch it; it was hair, blonde hair. It was wet, absorbing the moisture in the air I'm guessing. I continued to walk towards the brighter light wondering what was ahead.

After a few more feet, I came upon a small, round room with a spot light in one corner, I saw what looked like an electric box on one part of the wall, and a metal door that looked very heavy. I unlocked the door, turned the knob and pushed against it, forcing it open with a loud screeching sound. I was not sure what was beyond the door so I took a peek first, and then stepped out into the sun. I stepped out into a warm breeze, an ocean view and a gravel area with small sprouts of grass peeping through. I couldn't tell where I was so I climbed the small grassy hill that covered the entrance. When I got to the top, I could see our house, our boat and the city in the far distance. I stood for a bit, looking around, not really knowing what to think. My eyes started swelling up with tears of concern, trying to take in what I just experienced, and questioning why that area connects to our home.

I decided that I better go back the way I came. Walking as fast as I could, finally reaching the bookshelf. I peeked around the corner of it to take a look in a bid to make sure that I could get out of the secret passage way unnoticed. Good, nobody was there. I stepped out and pushed the shelving unit into the same position that I had found it. Before I left the room, I scrambled to make sure the room looked exactly the same. I did not want anyone asking me questions.

I headed back upstairs, cautiously looking around every corner. As I entered the foyer the doorbell rang. I jumped! The sound startled me, making my heart race. I looked at the door for a moment, then opened it.

"Hello," I said. "May I help you?"

A teenage girl with long black hair, beautiful blue-green eyes and a slim figure stood at the door.

"Hi, I need to speak to Esmeralda."

As soon as I started to respond, Esmeralda walked to the door quickly, clearly recognizing the girl at the door.

"Lucy! What are you doing here?" Esmeralda feeling thankful that Mr. Alatorre was not at home. He does not like it when uninvited people show up at his front door.

"I'm sorry mom but I didn't know what to do. I need your help."

I told Lucy to come inside so she could talk to her mother.

"You two go ahead and talk. I will leave." I said.

"Thank you Mrs. Alatorre." Esmeralda said.

As I walked away to give them their privacy, I could hear Esmeralda say to Lucy, "I told you to never come here no matter what. What if Mr. Alatorre sees you?" I noticed her voice got a little shaky. Esmeralda sounded nervous.

They stood in the foyer talking for a couple of minutes. As soon as they were finished, Esmeralda reached for the door to open it. To her surprise, Mr. Alatorre and some of his men were getting out of their cars. Making his way up the porch steps Mr. Alatorre said, "Well who do we have here?"

"Uhm. This is my daughter Lucy."

"No wonder I did not recognize her. I've only seen her once as a baby. I always forget you have a daughter Esmeralda." He said in a chilling tone.

"She was just leaving."

Esmeralda put her hand on Lucy's back and started pushing her out the door. She was nervously looking back and forth from Mr. Alatorre to Lucy, trying to use hand gestures and eye expressions to tell Lucy to keep walking. As Lucy was getting ready to walk past one of the men on the sidewalk, he quickly stepped in her path, stopping Lucy in her tracks. He smirked at her, raising one of his hands to touch her long black hair. Lucy, feeling threatened, slapped his hand away and took a step back.

Lucy was not afraid to stand up for herself. She is not easily intimidated; a trait she inherited from her father.

Esmeralda, wanting to distract Javier and his men, asked; "Did you come home for lunch? Can I make you some food Mr. Alatorre?"

"No Esmeralda, we have some business to take care of in my office." Javier turned to wave at his men to follow him and said, "By the way, you have a beautiful daughter. I'm sure her father is very proud."

"He is." Esmeralda said with a sickness in her stomach.

Glitch, the tall man with a mohawk and a scar on his face, said to Lucy, "Catch ya later," before he let her walk by. Lucy walked to her car, got in, looked out the window at her mom and took off. As Lucy drove away, Javier headed into the house with his men close behind.

Javier and his men walked down the hall in silence, entered into his office, then closed the door abruptly. Esmeralda had closed the front door behind the men but not before she took a quick look down the street to make sure Lucy was gone. She went back to cleaning the house as she does everyday.

After about an hour I decided to check on Esmeralda to see if Lucy was going to be okay. I walked into our bathroom to find Esmeralda sitting on the side of the bathtub with tears in her eyes, and a piece of tissue over her mouth as she lightly sobbed. I sat next to her, putting an arm around her shoulder, trying to let her know that I was there to support her. We both sat in silence for a moment while she let her sorrows out.

"Mrs. Alatorre I think I may need your help."

"Of course, what can I do?"

"Lucy confessed to me that she borrowed money from some bad people to help a friend. Lucy thought she would have no problem paying it back but apparently one day when she showed up to work, she found the doors bolted shut. They closed the restaurant she worked at without warning. She didn't tell me she lost her job. I......I......I don't know what to do, these people are threatening her."

"That's why she was here today? Do you know how much money she needs?"

"Twenty-five-hundred dollars. I'll do whatever it takes to pay you back if you could let me borrow it, but we can't let Mr. Alatorre find out. He can't find out for any reason, please."

I stood up, walking around the room, thinking of what to do. I don't have any cash here. If I take money out of our account, he will notice.

"I know Esmeralda, we will pawn some of my jewelry. This way, Javier won't know. We can go together, that way, nobody will question you. And if Javier notices the jewelry missing, I will just say I forgot where I put it."

Esmeralda stood up, walked over to me, grabbed both my hands, and looked at me, her eyes swelling up with tears.

"I don't know how to thank you." She said.

I grabbed her and hugged her. She meant a lot to me. She has been by my side since the accident and has treated me with nothing but warmth and tenderness. Helping to bring me back to life, teaching me, and patiently guiding me back into the world I had forgotten.

I leaned back away from her, putting my hands on both of her shoulders and said, "By the way this is a gift. You are not to worry about paying me back. I think Javier and I have enough money. I don't need you worrying about this."

"Thank you!"

We hugged each other again for a moment, though it felt like forever. I could feel the gratitude in her hug, nothing else needed to be said. We agreed to meet the next morning at her house, and that I would tell Javier that Esmeralda needed help shopping for some groceries and the car would be more convenient than Esmeralda taking the bus. That way, I could get out of the house without him questioning where I was and Esmeralda could be late for work just in case anything went wrong.

The rest of the day came and went. I was anxious for the morning to come. Fidgeting all night long while thinking about what the following day would bring. I wanted to help Lucy. I wanted Esmeralda to be happy again. She has been helping me recover, and I felt like I could use this opportunity to repay her.

The next morning, I grabbed a handful of jewelry, put it in a cloth jewelry bag, hid it in my purse and told Javier that I was heading to Esmeralda's house. As I turned onto Esmeralda's street, I could see her on the front porch waiting for me. She was looking back and forth, in anticipation of my arrival. When she saw me, she waved at me with one hand, while clutching her purse against her body with the other. She walked down the steps, gave me a little wave hello and jumped into the car.

"Good morning Mrs. Alatorre."

"Good morning, how are you feeling?"

"I'm doing well. Lucy and I talked last night. I told her our plans. She was very thankful for your help."

"Well, let's hope this works out. Did Lucy say when she was meeting up with these guys to pay them?"

"Yes, they have plans to meet tonight. I am worried about her meeting these people but she said she has a male friend who is going to go with her."

"Good, try and be positive." I drove away from her house, heading towards the city.

I was worried whether or not I brought enough jewelry, after all, I really didn't know the value of the pieces. I can only assume we would get enough money based on us being wealthy. Javier didn't seem like the type of man to buy fake jewelry.

We pulled into the parking lot of the Pawn shop, parked and sat for a moment discussing how to act inside.

"Okay," I said. "We need to walk in there with confidence. Don't let them see how amateurish we are, otherwise they will take advantage of us."

Esmeralda nodded in agreement. We both stepped out of the car and walked inside. We were the only ones there, probably because it was earlier in the morning. A younger man came out from the back of the store to help us. I told him we had some jewelry to sell as I started taking the jewelry out one piece at a time, waiting to hear his offer after each one. I didn't want him to see everything we had. After some negotiating we were able to get the amount of money we needed plus a little extra to help both Lucy and Esmeralda out for the next month or two. Walking out of the shop with our heads held high, we looked at each other not saying a word but knowing that we both were satisfied, that everything was working out so far. This was the first time since my accident that I truly felt alive. It was exciting! I felt like I was my own person again.

We got into the car and headed to the grocery store to complete our plan. Knowing that Javier would notice how long we were gone, we grabbed a few items quickly and headed to my house. I feared that if we were too late, Javier would start questioning us about what was taking so long. I didn't want to have to come up with a lie on the spot but my worries were for nothing because when we got home, I found a note from Javier. He had a problem at work and that he had to leave.

"Esmeralda, Javier isn't here!"

"This is a good sign. Now I just need to get the money to Lucy so she can get out of this mess." Esmeralda said.

I handed Esmeralda the money and told her to keep it safe until she leaves. I also insisted that she should leave early so that she could talk to Lucy and prepare her for the meet.

Esmeralda spent most of the day cleaning the kitchen and reorganizing the cabinets. I could tell she was trying to keep herself busy, to keep her mind off Lucy. Eventually she moved into Mr. Alatorre's office. Dusting, sweeping, vacuuming the small area rugs, but never cleaning Mr. Alatorre's desk. This was off limits. As she finished up, she walked towards the door to leave, her hands full of cleaning supplies, she noticed a small piece of paper on the floor lying between a table leg and a large, exquisitely painted vase. She stopped, let go of the vacuum, leaving it to stand upright so she could pick up the paper and stuff it into her apron pocket. But after she did this, she had a feeling rush over her body, an overwhelming feeling that she needed to look at the piece of paper. She reached into her pocket, unwrapped the scrunched up piece of paper to find a note saying,

"Next shipment is a top priority. Find only the prettiest girls."

She put the piece of paper back into her apron pocket, walked to the closet to put all the cleaning supplies away, grabbed her purse and walked around the house until she found me outside on the veranda drinking a glass of wine.

"Mrs. Alatorre, I'm leaving now."

I turned my head and saw Esmeralda walking towards me. I stood up and took a few steps to meet her.

"I'll drive you home. It'll be faster than catching the bus, not to mention the money in your purse."

"You have done enough for me. You don't have to do that."

As I started to walk past her, I took one of her hands and said, "Let's get you home." I could feel that her hand was shaking, and a little clammy. She was clearly feeling flustered, overwhelmed with apprehension. I felt like a mother protecting her child. Nothing was going to stop me from helping the woman who has helped me.

We drove home in almost complete silence. I think she could feel my determination in getting her home as soon as possible. I felt connected to her, like we were communicating telepathically.

Finally, we were almost at her house. I slowly pulled up along the curb and put the car in park. Turning my head, looking at her I said, "Please tell Lucy to be careful. I want you to call me when it's done. I need to know that she is safe."

She opened the door to get out. Before shutting the door, she looked over her shoulder and said to me, "I'll call you as soon as I can."

She tried to smile as best as she could. She closed the car door, walked up the steps to her house and went inside. I sat for a moment to take it all in, taking a deep breath and then finally driving back home thinking the entire time that her call won't come fast enough.

CHAPTER 7

"Lucy! Lucy are you home?" Esmeralda walked around the house looking for her but she was not home. The house felt quiet, eerily quiet. While she waited for Lucy, she decided to write down a plan. She wanted to make sure she did not forget anything she wanted to say to Lucy. Lucy has a tendency to be stubborn and strong-willed.

After about an hour Lucy walked in the front door.

"Mom?" She called out.

"I'm in the kitchen!"

"Did you get the money?"

"Yes. It's in my purse. Go grab it and count it. I don't want you to have any surprises tonight."

Lucy walked over to her mother's purse, picked it up and went to the kitchen table. She reached into the purse, took the money out and started counting.

"It's all here mom. Did you thank Mrs. Alatorre for me and tell her I will pay her back?"

"I did." Esmeralda turned around to talk directly to Lucy, "But she said it was a gift."

Lucy got up from the table and started to walk away. Esmeralda asked in shock, "Where are you going?"

"I'm just going to the bathroom mom."

"When you come back, we need to talk before you leave." Lucy went to the bathroom while Esmeralda sat down at the kitchen table to wait for Lucy. She was thinking about everything she wanted to say. She glanced across the table and saw her notes, reached out to grab them, read them over again to remind herself of her thoughts. While she was doing this, Lucy came back, sat down, waiting for her mom to speak. They started taking turns talking about the best way to handle tonight. Before long, their conversation was over. Esmeralda decided to wash the dirty dishes while Lucy got ready. Her friend will be picking her up soon. The friend that was going to help her tonight.

Lucy's cell phone buzzed softly, lighting up the screen just enough to get her attention. It was a text from her friend Alejandro Perez, the kid with the hoodie. It said he was outside waiting.

"I'm leaving mom, my friend's here."

Walking out of the door swiftly, she barely heard her mom say, "Be safe and text me when it's done!"

Lucy ran outside and hopped on the motorcycle her friend was driving. Putting on a helmet that was handed to her by Alejandro, she held onto his waist tightly in anticipation of a jolt when he took off. The two of them zoomed off into the dark, down a dimly lit street with only one good light on the main corner.

It is a warm, steamy night, you could feel the humidity in the air, the tension mounting as they got closer and closer to their final destination.

They finally made it into the city. Everywhere you looked, people were walking the streets. More and more cars started to back up, causing congestion on the roads. Alejandro started to weave in and out of them as they got closer to the bar. He pulled up in front of the Gringo Saloon, easily finding a place to park his motorcycle. They took off their helmets and locked them onto the bike so they wouldn't get stolen.

Lucy looked at Alejandro and said, "I'm glad to see there are a lot of people here."

"Yeah, witnesses." He said.

The Gringo Saloon stood tall, facing the ocean. It was a popular place among locals and tourists. It's a two story brick building with large glass windows to take in the ocean views. Edison lights were strung in a crisscross pattern over the patio area that was filled with patrons.

Lucy and Alejandro headed inside to look for their contact. As they walked through the smoke filled room, music was playing and people were talking loudly. Alejandro led the way through the crowd with Lucy close behind. They reached a large round table in the back corner of the bar that had two men and several ladies sitting at it. Alejandro recognized their contact right away, walked up to the table and nodded at him.

"You just made it in time, ese." Glitch pronounced in a rough voice while rubbing the scar on his face.

"We got the money." Alejandro said to him as he turned to retrieve it from Lucy.

"Here." Alejandro handed him the money that was wrapped in a small brown bag. "Are we good now?"

The scar-faced man handed the bag to his cohort at the table. While the money was being counted, Alejandro and Glitch stared each other down, trying to show each other they were not to be messed with.

The two men at the table nodded to each other. Glitch turned to Alejandro. "We're good. Remember my kindness and tell your girl she needs to worry about herself in this world."

He then looked at Lucy and said, "Catch ya later."

An eerie feeling came over Lucy. She heard that same, 'Catch ya later' phrase recently. Suddenly, her eyes got big, remembering it was one of Mr. Alatorre's men.

Alejandro grinned at the scar-faced man and walked away, grabbing Lucy's hand. Both of them walking out as fast as they could, pushing past people along the bar area, finally exiting the brick building. What a relief, it's over!

They sped away on the motorcycle but a few blocks down the road, Lucy tapped Alejandro on the shoulder. He pulled over to the side of the road while hearing Lucy say to him, "I need to call my mom. I'm sure she is worried."

Lucy called her mom to give her the good news. Both of them were safe and were heading back home. When

Esmeralda hung up the phone she immediately called me to let me know.

CHAPTER 8

A wrinkled hand of an old man pushed open a rustic wooden door. The creaking of the door caused all the patrons within the bar to turn their heads, wondering who was entering the watering hole for locals. Sun rays penetrated through the doorway, forcing some of the people within the light's beam to squint their eyes in disapproval.

The old man walked slowly inside, shutting the door behind him. The patrons inside embraced the cover of darkness once again. He walked to the back of the bar, taking uneven steps, saying hello to all he knew as he passed.

Javier was sitting in a booth that was shaped like a half circle, talking to his men. The old man saw him, and took his hat off just enough to tip it in recognition at Javier. He wobbled up to the closest bar stool, stumbled a bit and plopped down while trying to get the bartender's attention.

Javier stopped his conversation for a moment to make sure the old man made it onto his stool without falling. Satisfied with what he saw, he started talking again.

"I need someone branded and I want it done soon, quietly."

One of Javier's men; Glitch said, "Oh yeah! I know who you're talking about.......that dark-haired beauty at your house."

"Sí, Sí." Javier said as he lit a cigar. "She's special. I'm going to have private bids on her so we are going to do things a little different this time."

"We got this boss." Raul exclaimed.

"You know you can trust us." Glitch said while taking a sip of his beer.

Javier and his men continued to talk while drinking, trying to come up with a plan to brand Lucy without Esmeralda finding out about it. The men at the table were engulfed with adrenaline because of the payday coming their way. They decided to follow Lucy to learn about her habits, figure out the best time to grab her for branding. Javier told his men they had little time because the next shipment was coming up soon. They were to start that same day, in the middle of the night.

With every opening of the creaky wooden door, Javier could see that the sun was setting and the evening was upon them. The men had to end their celebration. Each man paid their bar bill, leaving one by one, walking to their cars over the cobble-stoned streets in the oldest part of town. Javier gave the bar owner a large tip before he left, thanking him for his hospitality.

Javier got home late but before he went to bed, he went into his office. Sitting in his desk chair, he turned on his computer to do some research but quickly noticed the desktop icon for his security camera system was blinking. He opened the file for the video footage of his office.

He sat for a moment watching what was taking place. He sat back into his chair, leaning on the arm of the chair with his hand reaching up to his forehead, rubbing it and then the side of his temple. Starting to get upset and not sure of what to do, Javier centered himself in the chair, turned to look out the window that was to his right, thinking about the past...

The yacht slowly bobbing up and down with the sea as they rolled around in bed, touching each other, experiencing each other's bodies for the first and only time. Making love without thought to the consequences later. Javier just wanting to satisfy his urges while his wife was out of town. The two of them holding each other in bed. Javier gently sliding one of his hands up and down her bare back, now feeling the shame of making love to Esmeralda. Feeling guilty that he used her so that he could feel better.

Knock. Knock. The door to the office moved slightly as I tapped it.

"Javie?" I said as I peeked through the small opening of the door.

Startled by the unexpected knocking on the door, he turned away from the window to look my way. "Hey, I'm just finishing up here."

I slowly opened the door, stepping into the doorway to lean against it while still holding the door knob.

"Is everything ok?"

"Nothing for you to worry about. Did I wake you?" Javier said as he closed his laptop, stood up, pushed his chair under his desk and started to walk my way.

"No, I was going to the restroom and saw the light."

When he reached me, he placed his hand on the door next to my hand. I could see by the expression in his eyes that he was perplexed by something but I have learned that if he is not ready to talk, he won't and so I decided to hold my tongue.

"Let's get my princess back to bed." He said in a whisper as he kissed me on my lips.

"No, let's get you to bed." I said softly while reaching for his hand to lead the way.

We got to our bedroom, Javier helped me back in bed and said he would be right back. I closed my eyes while rolling over to face the windows. It was such a beautiful night that I did not pull the curtains shut before going to bed. I had the long sliding wall of windows open to let the unusually cool air in. Hearing the crashing waves kept me calm, allowing me to fall asleep without the usual images racing in my head.

After a few minutes, Javier got into bed, also laying in the direction of the windows, with the moonlight accentuating the outline of his body as he laid there. He reached back with his right hand trying to find mine. As I reached for his, I scooted close to him, grabbing his hand, smelling his scent, our bodies in perfect sync with each other as we slowly drifted off to sleep.

In the meantime, Javier's two men, Glitch and Raul, sat in their SUV with the windows down, enjoying the cool air, while watching Lucy and Esmeralda's house for any sign of movement. Glitch and Raul have been Javier's henchmen the longest. Loyal and trustworthy to the core.

Glitch, a nickname given to him because of the hitch in his step when he walks, is a tall, skinny man. Raul is the complete opposite. He is on the shorter side, plump all over with long black hair that he always wears in a braided ponytail, covered with a cowboy hat that looks as if he just took it out of a trash bin.

They were parked just a few houses down from Esmeralda's. The expensive SUV stuck out like a sore thumb among all the older, run down cars on the street. Glitch was sitting in the driver's seat slouching, trying to hide his tall figure in the darkness, and carefully looking back and forth down the street. Raul was sitting in the passenger seat with his right arm dangling out of the window holding a cigarette that was half-smoked. The two men sat there for about an hour when Raul saw Lucy walking up the dark street in his side view mirror. Raul pulled his arm in the car slowly, reached over with his other hand towards Glitch and tapped on the center console to get his attention. Glitch looked over at Raul, nodded his head as if to say, get ready.

"We're just supposed to watch tonight." Glitch said.

"I know but there she is. We can't pass this opportunity up."

"The street has been very quiet so maybe it is a good time to do something." Glitch thought to himself. "Okay, let's do it."

As soon as Lucy got close enough, Raul jumped out of the car, grabbed her around her body with one hand while covering her mouth with the other. Glitch ran around the SUV and opened the door, the two men forcing Lucy inside. Raul held Lucy while Glitch ran around to the other side, sliding into the backseat, he pulled a gun out and said, "I told you I would catch ya later."

Lucy, remembering exactly who he was said, "What's going on? What do you want?" She was frantically looking between the two men so she could keep an eye on both of them. Raul, letting go of Lucy, pushed in a cigarette lighter knob that was on a small console directly in front of them.

"Listen carefully." Glitch said. "You are now the property of Mr. Alatorre. If you tell anyone about us branding you, especially your mother, we will kill her and you."

Lucy's eyes got wider and wider, realizing what was about to happen. Her eyes started to tear up while Raul reached for the lighter that masked as a branding tool. Glitch grabbed both of her hands while Raul pulled up her shirt slightly, exposing her stomach. He pushed the hot lighter with Mr. Alatorre's emblem on it into her skin just below her belly button. Lucy started screaming in pain. Raul reached up with his other hand to cover her mouth while the smell of her burnt skin was rising up into the air. She squirmed around in her seat as much as she could, trying to get away while still being restrained by Glitch.

"We will be watching you, so don't be stupid." Glitch said as he let go of her hands.

Lucy pulled her shirt over her stomach with one hand while wiping the tears off her face with the other, still feeling the intense pain pulsating under her shirt.

Raul opened the door, stepped out onto the sidewalk and gestured at Lucy to get out. She stepped out of the car, never making eye contact with him. She took a few steps down the street to maintain some distance between her and them. She eventually stopped to try to compose herself. She couldn't let her mom see her tears, her fear, her pain. Taking a few minutes to pull herself together, Lucy eventually went into the house. All the lights were already turned off except for the light over the stove. Luckily, her mom was already in her room asleep.

CHAPTER 9

I could not sleep the next several nights. I tossed and turned in bed repeatedly, graphic images were dancing in my head as if I was there in real life...

A man grabbed me from behind as he placed a white cloth over my mouth. I instinctively grabbed the man's arm, trying to escape his power, wiggling back and forth with my body trying to get leverage somehow. I could smell something sweet as I attempted to breathe in fresh air through the piece of cloth, knowing it was the wrong thing to do. I could feel my body getting weaker and weaker. I was unable to hold myself up anymore. The water in front of me became more and more blurry.

"Maria.......Maria......wake up." I could hear Javier's voice. It sounded so far away but I could feel him gently pushing on my shoulder trying to wake me up. Startled by his touch, my body jerked a little as I woke up trying to figure out where I was.

"Are you okay?"

"Yes. It was just a dream." I said with a deep sigh.

"I'm going to stay home so I can be there for your appointment with Dr. Ruiz."

"It's not necessary Javie. I'm fully capable of talking to him myself."

Javier sat up in bed, turned to put his feet on the ground, sitting on the edge, and looking out the window.

"I know but I will feel better if I am there with you."

I didn't feel like arguing. He's as stubborn as an ox so I knew there was no point.

We both got ready for the day. Dr. Ruiz was coming this morning so we had little time to do other things. Javier spent the morning in his office on his computer, probably rescheduling work meetings. I walked around the house, fumbling through things. Just aimlessly wandering around because I still could not stop thinking about the dream I had. Eventually, I came upon Esmeralda, who was cleaning as usual but I interrupted her to talk. I was worried about my test results so I thought that maybe she could calm me down.

"How are you and Lucy doing?" I asked.

"Oh. Hello Mrs. Alatorre." She said as she stopped dusting for a moment. "We are doing good thanks to you. How are you feeling?"

"I had a bad dream last night. They are becoming more and more vivid, too real in fact."

"Sometimes dreams are trying to tell you something and sometimes they are just your mind being creative. Are you taking your medicine properly?"

"Yes, Javier thinks that maybe Dr. Ruiz needs to change my dosage."

"Mrs. Alatorre, it's none of my business but I care about you. Your help with Lucy can never be repaid but I think you should stop taking the medicine and see what happens. Maybe the medicine is not good for you."

"But they may help me remember."

"Then just talk to Dr. Ruiz and see what he says before making any other decisions. He is the best doctor in town. Mr. Alatorre would only hire the best doctor take care of you."

"You're right. I'll let you get back to work. Dr. Ruiz should be here soon anyway."

Esmeralda winked at me and started dusting again. As I started to walk down the hallway towards the living room, I could hear Javier and Dr. Ruiz talking. I was so engrossed in my conversation with Esmeralda that I didn't even hear the doorbell ring. As I got closer I could hear them talking about me having dreams.

"I don't think the medicine is working anymore." Javier said with a worried tone in his voice.

"You know this is experimental. Let me talk to her and see what is going on." Dr. Ruiz said with confidence.

I stopped in my tracks when I heard this. I did not want them to see me. I did not want them to know that I heard what they had said. I quietly slipped into a bathroom that was thankfully in the right place at the right time.

I tried my best to listen in but it was much harder to hear in the bathroom. I could only hear bits and pieces. Javier clearly was concerned about me getting my memories back. I was lost in my thoughts; "Was Esmeralda right? Maybe I should stop taking the medicine. I am so confused. Why would my husband not want me to remember? Is there something he is hiding from me? Maybe he doesn't want me to remember the horrors of the accident?" I didn't have the answers to anything but I decided to interrupt them by walking out of the bathroom loudly. I flushed the toilet, washed my hands and pretended that I never heard them.

"Javier is that you?" I said as I walked quickly down the hallway, making sure to have confidence in my voice.

"Yes, Dr. Ruiz is here."

I approached Dr. Ruiz with a smile on my face and an open hand ready to shake. "How are you? We appreciate you coming all the way out here today."

"Of course," he said. "Nothing I wouldn't do for my favorite patient. Why don't we sit on the couch so we can talk?" He gestured with his hand, pointing towards the living room.

We all made our way into the living room. Dr. Ruiz and I sitting on the couch next to each other while Javier sat in a chair nearby. Dr. Ruiz did his normal examination, making sure my vitals were normal, my throat, eyes and ears looked good.

"So Mr. Alatorre tells me you have been having some vivid dreams lately," he said.

"I'll admit they have been a little too real."

"But other than that, you feel good?"

"Yes."

"It seems that your body may be getting used to the medication. I'm going to give you a higher dosage for a week or two and see if it calms your mind."

"Will I have to take this for the rest of my life Dr. Ruiz?"

"I can't determine that yet but it's always a possibility. You have been through a major accident that affected your brain. I am going to do whatever it takes to keep you healthy, to live a normal life."

"I understand. Javie picked a great doctor. I trust you."

Surprisingly Javier was quiet. I guess I said all the right things otherwise he would have chimed in. I looked his way with a smile on my face when the entire time, I was truly worried about what I heard. I decided to go along with all of this so they would not be suspicious. Dr. Ruiz fiddled in his bag for a moment and then pulled out a new bottle of medicine.

"You will take this the same as the other bottle. Nothing changes but the dosage. I want you to pay attention to whether you feel it is helping and then I will put it in my plans to talk to you in about a week so I'll know how you respond to it."

"I will Dr. Ruiz." I started to stand up to indicate that I was done talking.

Javier and the doctor also stood up. Javier thanked Dr. Ruiz for his time while shaking his hand, then walked him to the front door. I stood there waiting to see if they would go outside to talk but Javier must have been satisfied. As he closed the door, I started to walk towards him not saying anything. When he turned towards me, he noticed me approaching so he met me half way.

"Dr. Ruiz is in the top of his field. Listen to him and everything will be fine." Javier said as he kissed me on my cheek.

"I know."

"I'm going to grab some things from my office and head to work. I'll see you tonight."

"See you tonight." I needed to think. I decided to walk down by the water so I could be alone.

In the meantime, Esmeralda, given permission to take half the day off, was finished for the day and ready to go home to see Lucy. She walked by Javier's office but it wasn't fast enough.

"Esmeralda!" Javier yelled as he saw her walk by.

Her body cringed when she heard her name being called. She was so focused on going home, she did not notice the office door was open. She turned around, put her cleaning box on the floor outside and stepped into the room.

"Yes, Mr. Alatorre?"

"Shut the door. I need to talk to you."

Esmeralda shut the door as requested, fearing what was coming her way because of the tone in his voice.

"Esmeralda we have known each other for a very long time. I want you to tell me the truth. Were you in my office not too long ago and found a note?"

How did he know I found a note? She thought. Esmeralda had a feeling she already knew what this would be about, Lucy. Girls that are as beautiful as Lucy would one day be scouted by Javier and his men. She was hoping that the vast distance between her home and Javier's would keep her daughter safe but Lucy made the mistake of coming to the Alatorre's home and now, Esmeralda has to fight.

"Yes, I found a note." She answered.

"Just to make myself clear, I will do anything when it comes to my business."

"Why are you telling me this?"

"You know why." He stared at her intensely.

"My daughter is off limits!"

Javier looked at her surprised. He was not used to seeing this side of Esmeralda, especially as she was talking back at him with such force. He walked right up to Esmeralda, staring her in the eyes, trying to intimidate her. His large stature overwhelming her small, plump figure.

"Do not interfere Esmeralda or there will be consequences for you too." He said without blinking an eye.

Esmeralda knew then and there that she was never coming back to work. She turned to walk out the door, fuming inside, knowing that the days ahead would be the most challenging days of her life.

CHAPTER 10

The Mazatlán Cathedral is a beautiful church with a Baroque-Revival style façade, and two bell towers flanked on each side. Located in the city's historical center, it is surrounded by a wrought iron fence and gate to protect its heritage.

I pushed open the wooden door, softly taking each step over the black and white checkered floor, looking around for Esmeralda. The church is lined with wooden pews and concrete pillars that rise majestically to the exquisite roof. Looking around in amazement, I quickly remembered why I was here. I saw Esmeralda about halfway down the aisle in a pew by herself. I sat down next to her. Her eyes were closed, praying.

"Esmeralda?" I tapped her on her leg gently. She finished her prayer quickly and turned her body towards me while looking around to see if we had privacy.

"Thank you for coming."

"What's going on? Why are you not at work?"

"I quit last night. I wanted you to hear it from me Mrs. Alatorre." She said as she dipped her head looking down at the white handkerchief she held in her hand.

"Why? What can I do to change your mind?"

"I can't thank you enough for all that you have done to help Lucy and me. I wanted you to know that, just in case I never get to see you again." She said with tears building up in her eyes.

"Never see me again. We can still see each other. I need you." I said in despair.

She reached into her purse while sniffling back her runny nose. Pulling out a picture, she handed it to me and said.

"For you to remember me and our relationship." It was a picture of Esmeralda and me from a long time ago. We were both on a beach in our swimsuits, making funny faces for the camera.

"Esmeralda…..I…..I…..don't know what to say." I started tearing up, knowing how much I would miss her and knowing how lonely I would be without her.

She reached up to gently wipe away a tear rolling down my face. "I need to tell you one more thing. You must stop taking those pills from Dr. Ruiz. They are suppressing your memories. Stop immediately and the truth will come out." She suddenly grabbed me, hugged me tightly, squeezing with all her heart, then turning to leave the pew.

"Esmeralda wait! Please!" I yelled passionately. My voice echoing throughout the church. I was completely confused and heartbroken.

I watched the only friend I had walk out that church without looking back.

Sitting in silence, I watched an older woman several pews in front of me praying loudly for a sick family member. I found myself starting to pray too. This was the first time I had been in a church since my accident. Maybe I was there for a reason, because everything in my life seemed to be going backwards instead of forward. I prayed for Esmeralda, Lucy and Javier. I asked for the strength to trust Esmeralda's word, to stop taking my medicine.

After I finished praying, I looked down at the photograph that was lying on my lap. I picked it up and noticed a dark mark underneath my belly button, but it was hard to pinpoint what it was. Was it dirt? I do not have a mark like that under my belly button. It was too small to see with the naked eye so I put the photo away in my purse and headed home.

As I walked to my car, I couldn't help but muster a half smile at the locals socializing with each other and a few of the tourists who were also wandering around. Everyone seemed happy and content. The street vendors were either selling their handmade art or their home grown vegetables. Life seemed easy and uncomplicated; the opposite of what I was feeling.

When I got home, the house seemed so quiet, so empty. I felt so alone but I knew I couldn't feel sorry for myself. I was on a mission, so I went into the kitchen where we had a built-in desk with drawers. I was hoping to find a magnifying glass to look at the photo more closely. Searching each drawer carefully, moving papers, pens and pencils, greeting cards, I eventually found it!

Taking the photo and the magnifying glass over to the kitchen island, I saw what could only be described as a tattoo. It was some kind of symbol that I had never seen before. Second guessing myself, I lifted up my shirt to look; nothing. I ran my fingers over the area to see if it was rough, maybe a remnant of a tattoo I used to have, nothing. I have looked at so many photo albums lately but I do not remember seeing a tattoo in other pictures of me in a bikini. There are plenty of pictures of Javier and myself on our yacht but I do not recall seeing a tattoo.

I decided to call Ava.

"Hi Ava it's Maria."

"Hello Maria. How are you? I haven't heard from you in a while."

"I know. I guess I have been keeping myself busy lately. I wanted to ask you for a favor." I said inquisitively.

"Absolutely. I will do whatever I can to help."

"I am going to start a project for Javier's birthday. I need some older photos of us together on our yacht trips. I am putting together a collage for him and was hoping you had some older photos I can use. I am kind of making a timeline thing and I do not have older photos of us together here at the house. At least I cannot find any. Could you help me out by texting some to me?"

"I should have some I think. I will go through my pictures tonight if that's okay and send any that I may have later."

"Sounds great! I really appreciate your help. This is a surprise so don't tell anyone." I said, trying not to sound suspicious.

"Sure. Talk to you later."

"Bye."

I felt terrible lying to her but with Esmeralda telling me to stop taking my medicine so that the truth can come out, along with the old photograph I was lucky to come by, my gut was telling me to pursue this.

Later in the afternoon, I realized that Esmeralda wasn't home to make dinner so I went to the refrigerator to see what I could possibly make. I had not tested my cooking skills on my own yet so the little experiment was likely to go awry. I looked in the refrigerator to see what type of ingredients we had, then I used a recipe book to help me concoct a meal.

By the time Javier got home, I had made a huge mess but accomplished my goal. My first cooked meal. I set the table outside on the veranda. Javier and I have not had a relaxing evening together in a while. He had been very busy at work lately, coming home later and later every day. Tonight though was just the two of us.

Just as I was about to go find Javier, he walked into the kitchen.

"Oh my goodness did a hurricane hit us!" He said jokingly.

"Apparently! Hey, I did my best."

He walked over to give me a hug and kiss.

"Thank you for all your efforts. I am sure dinner will be delicious."

"We're about to find out." I said with a slight giggle while pointing to the table outside. "Let's eat!"

We sat down at the table, eating, drinking and talking about our day but never mentioning that I saw Esmeralda.

"Did Esmeralda say why she quit?" I asked.

"No, not really. She said something about being tired of the long travel time to get here."

"I don't blame her but I will miss her. She has helped me a lot."

"Maybe she will come back soon." He said, looking directly in my eyes.

When we were done with dinner, I cleaned up the kitchen while Javier responded to a voicemail he got while we were eating. It was a Friday night so we decided to relax by watching a movie and cuddling.

Towards the end of the movie, Javier had dozed off into dream land. I knew he was tired from working so I let him sleep. It was the right move because Ava sent me a text with several pictures of us from when we were younger. As soon as I saw them, I got up from the couch and headed outside. There it is, proof. Several of the pictures with me in it had that same tattoo under my belly button. It was not dirt. It was not a black smudge but a real tattoo that now does not exist.

One of the pictures was pretty clear so when I zoomed in I could see the symbol more clearly. It took me a moment to realize what it was. It was the Zodiac sign for Gemini. The symbol for twins. Just when things started to feel normal my life had become questionable.

The next day, Javier told me he had to go on a work trip so I thought it would be a good time to take Esmeralda's advice and stop my medicine. That way, I would not have to hide it from Javier and lie if he noticed. After a day or two, I did not feel much of a difference. My headaches seemed to be the same, which is odd because the medicine was supposed to keep them under control. The entire time, I kept wondering, "Shouldn't they get worse?"

I decide to go one more night without them. I got into Javier's side of the bed that night. I had our sliding doors open again because it was such a beautiful night. Javier doesn't like them open so I decided to take advantage of him not being home to do what I wanted. Plus, like I said before, the sound of the waves crashing against the rocks keeps me calm. I needed that serenity especially that night because my mind was racing, wreaking havoc on my ability to fall asleep but eventually I dozed off...

A man grabbed me from behind as he placed a white cloth over my mouth. I instinctively grabbed the man's arm, trying to escape his power, wiggling back and forth with my body, trying to get leverage somehow. I could smell something sweet as I attempted to breathe in fresh air through the piece of cloth, knowing it was the wrong thing to do. I could feel my body getting weaker and weaker. The man gently turned me around while trying to keep me on my feet the best he could.

"I'm sorry! I'm sorry! I don't know what else to do!"

"Why? I don't understand Josh!"

I looked around in a daze, feeling confused and desperate. My legs starting to feel weak. Unable to hold my body up anymore I fell into the chair next to me. Opening my eyes, closing my eyes, feeling the heaviness of them while trying to watch what was taking place.

I could hear a boat approaching ours. As the motor noise got louder and louder, Josh walked over to the side of our yacht to help them tie up. A scruffy-looking man boarded our boat, looked over at me, and then handed a duffle bag to my husband. Two other men, who were also standing on the boat deck, dropped four more bags next to his feet.

"There's the money that was agreed upon." The scruffy man said with a thick accent.

He walked towards me pulling something out of his pants pocket. I could hardly tell what was going on anymore. I was barely conscious. But before I completely passed out, I could feel a prick in my arm. He injected me with something.

His two sidekicks then took over, picking me up and taking me to their boat. Josh just stood there, rubbing his forehead, doing his best not to watch while I was taken away. The boat with me aboard drove off into the distance, getting smaller and smaller against the horizon.

Josh couldn't move. He was paralyzed with what he had just done.

"I'm sorry Maia.......I'm so sorry." He said softly into the blowing wind that was not listening.

I woke up sweating, breathing heavily from the vividly realistic dream. Looking around desperately trying to figure out where I was, feeling as if I was on the boat myself, a loud bang from thunder outside my bedroom windows woke me up.

I got out of bed to close the sliding doors so the rain wouldn't come inside. As I shut the last door, I became mesmerized by the lightening flashing in the distant sky; with my heart pounding while remembering what Esmeralda had said to me.

Stop the pills and the truth will come out.

CHAPTER 11

Javier told me he was going on a work trip but he was actually in town preparing for a special auction. His men were getting ready for an in-person auction which he never does. Usually, the girls are sold in a small group to one person. A buyer would have a middleman who would then pay for the girls, pick them up and deliver them but this time, Javier wanted the buyers to all be in one location, hoping the face to face competition would entice the bids to get as high as possible. However, the auction could not start without the prize.

"Glitch, I need you and Raul to get Lucy tonight." Javier said.

"We're on it Boss." Glitch said while rubbing the scar on the side of his face.

"Remember, do not grab her in front of Esmeralda. That will be a problem for us. I want Lucy out of the country before Esmeralda finds out. Then I will deal with her."

"Understood." Glitch waved at Raul to follow him so they could go find Lucy.

Lucy was able to get a new job working at a local gas station. Since Glitch and Raul had been tracking her, they decided to start by looking for her at her work.

It was late in the afternoon. Lucy doesn't usually go to work until the evening so they decided to wait in their SUV. They parked along the street that was the opposite of the gas station, far enough down to not get noticed, but close enough to see if Lucy showed up. While sitting in their SUV, they made their plans, knowing that the best time to approach her would be later in her shift when she would take out the trash. The darkness, the lack of people and Lucy's inattentiveness would benefit them.

After a couple of hours, Raul spotted Lucy getting out of a car driven by Esmeralda; a car she borrowed from a friend.

"Hey!" Tapping Glitch on his leg. "There she is."

Glitch watched Esmeralda sit in her car for a minute or two while Lucy entered the gas station safely. Eventually driving away, Lucy was now on her own. The two men sat patiently waiting; smoking, drinking and eating as if they were on an official stakeout. As the evening went on, the gas station customers became less and less frequent, creating a perfect scenario for Glitch and Raul.

Raul exited the passenger side of the SUV and walked across the street. There was a dark area of the parking lot where the trash dumpster stood. This is where they planned on making their move. Raul stood under the cloak of the darkness, keeping aware of his surroundings, patiently waiting.

About an hour later, someone had turned on the outside door light. It was dim and flickered continuously, begging for someone to put in a new bulb. A rustling noise could be heard on the other side of the door as if someone was preparing to open it. Click, click. Locks were being disabled and the door knob started to turn. Someone pushed up against the door that was clearly suffering from rust and old age. When the door opened, Raul could see it was Lucy. She propped the door open with a brick that was nearby so it would not accidentally lock her out.

Raul took a glance down the street at the SUV to see if Glitch was paying attention. He could see him slowly pulling out of the parking spot with no head lights on, heading towards him. When Raul saw that they were on the same page, he stepped out from the darkness to grab Lucy.

Glitch pulled into the parking lot directly in front of the garbage bin, getting as close as he could so they could be as quick as possible. Raul held Lucy around her waist with one hand while covering her mouth with the other. She was kicking and screaming the best she could, trying to prevent him from putting her into the SUV.

Out of nowhere, another car pulled up behind the SUV blocking it in. Esmeralda jumped out of the front seat with a gun, pointing at Raul and Lucy.

"Let her go!" She said as her hand was shaking ever so slightly.

Esmeralda had been secretly watching Lucy at work. She knew that Javier's men would come for her soon. She would drop Lucy off, act like she was heading home, only to turn around a couple of blocks down the street, parking in very discrete locations so she could watch Lucy and the surrounding area, never parking in the same spot twice.

"Back off lady!" Raul said as he was still trying to handle Lucy.

Just then, Glitch stepped out of the vehicle pointing a gun at Esmeralda.

"Put the gun down! I don't want to hurt you!"

Esmeralda, not caring about what happens to her, ran towards Lucy. Glitch put his gun in its holster and quickly ran towards Esmeralda, trying to stop her from interrupting the kidnapping.

"Stop! Stop! Let her go!" Esmeralda screamed as she reached the two of them fighting by the SUV.

Raul somehow managed to get the car door open during this confrontation. Just as Esmeralda started to lift her gun again, Glitch grabbed her from behind in a bear hug and reached for her gun. They struggled for a few seconds before Glitch finally got the gun out of Esmeralda's hand. While Raul managed to get Lucy into the back seat and shut the door, Glitch threw Esmeralda to the ground and walked away, remembering that Javier said not to hurt her.

Just as Esmeralda was able to get to her feet, Glitch backed up the large SUV into Esmeralda's car in an effort to get away, pushing her car to go back far enough to get out of the parking spot, and causing the left tire to pop and go flat.

They drove away, screeching tires and smoke filling the air, as Esmeralda watched in horror. Screaming as her only daughter disappeared into the night.

While driving down the city streets, Raul tied Lucy's hands and put a black cloth bag over her head so she could not see where they were going.

The three of them drove for a while, traveling out of the city and into the countryside where Javier had a rustic hideaway for his men, himself and his business ventures.

The cabin was not very large but it had an impressive wrap around porch from the front to the back and was made out of wood from the surrounding trees. The inside had high-vaulted ceilings with several large support beams that looked like real trees growing out of the ground. It was decorated with a mix of leather and wood furniture, some with wrought iron details.

When they arrived, a few of Javier's men came out to meet them. Raul escorted Lucy inside to meet Javier with Glitch not far behind. The two men who came out to meet Raul and Lucy stayed outside to keep a look out.

Raul helped Lucy sit in a nearby chair, then he took off the black hood she was wearing. Lucy immediately looked around the room, with her face lightly covered with sweat because of the hood being on for so long. She watched Raul and Glitch walk over to another man who was standing by a bar area with a gun on his hip and a drink in his hand. After a few minutes, a handsome middle-aged man with a scruffy beard and an expensive suit walked into the room and sat on the edge of a chair next to Lucy.

"Do you know who I am?" Javier asked.

"Yes, you are my mother's boss."

"This is true but I am also a business man who gives beautiful young ladies such as yourself a better life. Would you like a better life?"

"Take me back home. I am not interested in what you have to say."

Javier slowly leaned back into his seat, relaxing, staring at Lucy before responding.

"A friend of mine, her name is Ava, will be here tomorrow to help you get ready for an auction we are having on my private island. You my dear, are the prize and you will cooperate. If you do not, I have ways to make sure you do."

Javier got up from his chair without waiting for a response. Lucy's instinct was to try and run but if she tried her efforts would be stopped immediately.

"My men will show you to your room." Javier signaled for his men to take her away.

Raul and Glitch walked over to Lucy and escorted her to a room down the hall. When she stepped into the room, she first noticed that there was no window. She saw a small table with a plate of food, a drink and a vase of flowers directly across the room. As she glanced around, she could see that the room was clearly decorated for a girl. To the left was a wrought iron bed, flanked by small tables and lamps. To the right was a TV mounted on the wall, a closet and a bathroom.

Sitting down on the edge of the bed, Lucy started bopping one leg up and down out of anxiety. Her mind racing uncontrollably. Thinking about whether her mom was hurt, whether she would ever see her mom again and how she was going to get out of this situation. Lucy tried hard to keep her tears at bay, she rarely cried.

It was late at night and Lucy was tired, tired from working her job and all the chaos. Turning her body to lay on the bed with her shoes left on, she eventually nodded off.

The next morning, Lucy was awakened by a knock on the door. The door slowly opened making a few creaking sounds as it moved. Ava stuck her head in the room, trying to maintain some privacy for Lucy, and said, "Lucy are you awake?"

Rolling over from her side to her back, Lucy rubbed one of her eyes that would not focus so she could see who was at the door. She reluctantly sat up in the bed, grabbing a pillow and putting it in front of her as if it was a protective shield.

"Hi, I'm Ava." She started to walk into the room, getting closer to Lucy. "I am going to be with you for the rest of your journey."

Lucy didn't say anything to her. She just watched Ava.

"Today I am going to help you get dressed, put on some makeup and do your hair. We need to make an impression, a next level impression."

"You can talk all you want but I am not going with you." Lucy exclaimed.

"I will give you some privacy to take a shower. I will be back in thirty minutes." Ava said as she walked out the door.

Lucy got out of bed a few minutes later and started pacing back and forth, eventually doing what she was told.

Ava knocked on the door again and entered the room with a syringe in her hand. Glitch walked in behind her and headed straight for Lucy. Lucy started screaming at them to stay away, trying her best to get away but Glitch was too fast and strong. As Glitch held Lucy in place, Ava injected a liquid into her arm.

As the drug started to take effect, Glitch sat Lucy on the bed so she could regain her composure. In the meantime, Ava started to get out the items she needed to help get Lucy ready for the auction. Glitch left the room, closed the door behind him but stood outside just in case Ava needed his help again.

Ava and Lucy spent the next hour in the room without an incident. When they were finally ready, Ava called out to Glitch to come into the room to help her get Lucy in the car and to the island.

Once they were all in the car, Ava called Javier. "Javier, we just left the house. We should reach the island in about three hours."

"Did you have any problems?" Javier asked.

"Unfortunately, we did have to drug her." Ava responded.

"All right. Keep me up to date as you make your way here. The clients should be arriving in an hour."

"Sounds good." Ava hung up the phone and told Glitch that everything was on schedule.

The three of them made their way to the boat dock where Javier's yacht was waiting, along with a few more men. All of them boarded the yacht. While Ava put Lucy in a cabin room, Glitch and the other men prepared the boat for launching, then sailed off.

The island was surrounded by a white sandy beach, scattered palm trees and a large modern home that was made out of almost entirely glass to enjoy the immense views. The landscaping was exquisitely manicured to match the beauty of the island.

As they were approaching the island, Ava called Javier one more time to let him know that they would be ready for the auction soon. Ava and Glitch escorted Lucy off the boat and into what can only be described as a pool house. Ava noticed that the drug was wearing off because Lucy was more functional now; good timing indeed. It was necessary for her to be conscious because of what was about to happen.

Late afternoon was approaching as Javier's guests started to gather by the swimming pool. Men from all over the world chatting with each other, sizing each other up, some friends and some enemies. The pool was covered by a floor that appeared to be glass. Along the edges of the pool were LED lights changing colors to set the mood.

A tinging of a glass could be heard amongst the crowd before Javier told his guests to have a seat. Each man took a seat designated for them so they could bid on Lucy when she came out.

"Welcome everyone. Tonight is a special night. We have an exceptional product for you. She is a beautiful, very feisty young lady who will not disappoint." Javier bolstered. "Our rules remain the same as always, except this time you will be bidding out loud one at a time, in order for fairness."

The group of men looked around at each other with excitement as Javier walked over to the pool house to check on Ava and Lucy.

"We're ready Ava." Javier said, after opening the door and stepping into the doorway.

"We are too. I will send her out in one minute."

Javier nodded at Ava and headed back outside. Ava helped Lucy get off the couch she was sitting on; her legs were still a little woozy from the drugs. They walked to the door, where Ava stopped and told Lucy what to do when she got outside.

"Lucy look at me." Ava gently took her chin and moved it upward so that they can see each other eye to eye. "I am going to walk you to the pool and then stop at the edge. You are going to walk onto the pool cover into the center area and wait there until you see Mr. Alatorre wave at you. Do you understand?"

"Yes."

"Do not mess this up or there will be consequences after. Remember, the safety of your mother can change."

"I understand." Lucy said reluctantly but she knew there was no way out of this so she would not jeopardize her mother's life too. She loved her mother too much.

As they exited the small house and made their way to the pool, the approval of the men could be heard clearly. Javier smirked with excitement when hearing this. He knew Lucy would bring in the most money for a single girl since he entered the world of human trafficking.

Ava directed Lucy to walk to her spot for the auction and Lucy did just that. Looking around at all the men, she stood there feeling violated by their eyes. She was in high heel shoes, something she was not use to wearing, a soft, lacy floor length dress that was practically see through. Her long black hair, styled with beach waves and a hair clip to match her dress held back one side, while the other side seductively covered one of her green eyes.

"Lucy everyone!" Javier announced while pointing towards her. "We will start bidding with Mr. Sato then make our way around. Each of your chairs are equipped with a button for a green light and red light. All lights will start on green. If you wish to opt out or stop bidding just press your red button and we will skip you until a winner is announced."

"Mr. Sato whenever you are ready." Javier gestured towards him and took a bow out of respect.

The bidding started at a very high sum of Fifty-Thousand dollars. It continued for quite some time before Javier's guests starting dropping out one by one. The final two men went back and forth, sometimes taking long pauses in between to decide if they wanted to move forward. Finally, Mr. Sato won the game. Mr. Sato was an extremely rich Asian man who was not exactly easy on the eyes. His business was to use the women he bought for breeding purposes, selling babies and eventually, the women when they could not produce anymore; but not Lucy. Lucy was to be his bride.

As the night started to wind down, the group of men began to say their goodbyes. Some were being picked up by their private helicopters, others were to leave by boat but the only one invited to stay the night was the winner, Mr. Sato. Javier hosted the winner to say thank you and to talk about future business before taking Lucy back to his home country the next day.

CHAPTER 12

"CLARITY IN MY LIFE"

I decided that I would try to find Esmeralda and hopefully talk one more time. But I was interrupted by the usual conversations I would hold in my head. "Was it too late?" The problem was that I really didn't know where to start. "Would she still be at her house or has she left town?" The only thing I could do was check the places that I had seen her. "Who knows, maybe one of her neighbors would know something," I decided. Since she picked the church where we met, maybe someone there would know her. I needed to find a picture of her and luckily, there was one that I saw in a photo album on the living room shelf. I needed one to show how she looks now, not the one she gave me in the church when we were younger.

Javier was supposed to come back that same day so I had at least a couple of hours to investigate and hopefully, find her. I grabbed the photograph and my purse and headed out. Driving cautiously because of my nerves, but still remaining aware of my limited time.

I started with her house. After parking my car, I walked up to her door, knocking feverishly so it would catch her attention. Nobody answered the door. I turned around to go next door when I noticed an older man walking a dog.

"Sir! Excuse me sir! I am looking for my friend who lives in this house. This is her." I pointed to Esmeralda in the photo. "Do you know her?"

"I've seen her around but not lately ma'am. Is everything okay?"

"No, she is missing. Do you happen to know any of her friends or relatives that I can talk to?"

"I don't know her well enough to say." The old man said with empathy. "I know she has a daughter and sometimes, she sits on that porch over there with another girl. Maybe she will know."

"I will go see, thank you."

Since he pointed out a specific neighbor, I thought that would be the next best option. I walked across the street, approached the house that had a barking dog inside and knocked on the door. A cute little toddler answered the door, followed by a girl that looked about the same age as Lucy.

"Can I help you?" She said in a cautious voice, wondering who I was.

"Hi. Sorry to bother you but one of your neighbors told me you may know Lucy and Esmeralda. I am trying to find them."

"I haven't seen either of them." She said as she tried to close the door.

"Please! I think they are missing. Can you tell me anything?"

"I know Lucy. She is a friend of my cousin Alejandro. They hang out quite a bit. Talk to him." She clearly was trying to get rid of me; standing there while swirling a finger around one of the curls in her hair, while trying to shut the door on me.

"Wait! Can you tell me where he lives?"

The girl walked away leaving the front door ajar signaling she would be back. After a minute or two, she handed me a scrap piece of paper with his address.

"Thank you. I appreciate your help." She quickly shut the door. I could hear her yelling at the dog to be quiet and go lay down.

Not knowing the area well enough, I had to stop at a local gas station to ask for directions. Luckily he did not live far away so it was easy to find. It was an apartment complex located in a rundown neighborhood. Trash littered the streets, weeds grew out of cracked sidewalks and graffiti was painted on most of the crumbling buildings. I feel terrible that people have to live this way while I have everything that I desire. It made me wake up to the reality of Esmeralda and Lucy's hard life.

With the scrap piece of paper in my hand, and my purse tightly tucked under an arm, I walked quickly and non-discretely into the complex to look for his apartment. Luckily, today I was dressed in blue jeans and a t-shirt which is not my usual style but I at least felt like I blended in with the community better.

Not all of the apartments had their numbers hanging on the door but from what I could tell, the door I stood in front of should be his. I knocked with hope. The door opened for which I was thankful because I didn't have anywhere else to go to but to the church.

"Hello. My name is Maria Alatorre. Are you Alejandro?"

"That's me. Your last name sounds familiar." He stated.

"Your cousin gave me your name. She said you know Lucy Garcia. I am really looking for her mother but I was hoping you could help me since you know Lucy."

"Yeah I know Lucy, she's kind of my girl." He said proudly and with a smirk.

"Have you seen either of them lately? I need to talk to her mother. It's important."

"Naw. Lucy said they had to go out of town for a bit. Haven't seen her for days."

"Did she say where?" I kept pushing him for answers.

"She's been rattled lately. She had to pay money to some bad dude with a mohawk and a scar. I knew she wanted to get out of town because she was scared so I never asked."

"Wait......what? Was his name Glitch?"

"Yeah, I think that's the dude's name."

"Do you have a pen? I want to give you my number so you can call me when she comes back." He went to get a pen. I gave him my number, thanked him and left.

Glitch was the one she owed money to? I didn't see Glitch very often but he had always made me feel uncomfortable. The man always has a smirk on his face and stares at you, like his mind is running wild with ideas of what he wants to do to you.

My next stop was the church in town. As I drove there, I kept a close eye on the clock. I had to manage my time because it was going by fast. Getting back before Javier was a priority.

As I entered the church, I glanced around quickly at first, hoping to see Esmeralda but she was not in sight. I decided to walk around, with picture in hand, to see if there were any staff around or a Priest I could speak with. I made my way through some small hallways that ended up leading me back into the Nave of the church. I stood in the corner of the church by the doorway where I had just exited from, when I noticed a lady who was sitting in a pew that looked familiar. I think she was there the day I spoke to Esmeralda. "If she spends a lot of time in this church maybe she knows Esmeralda," I thought. I headed over to sit next to her.

She was a tiny, older lady with grey hair that she covered with a multi-colored scarf. Her face was completely covered with deep wrinkles. Her eyes recessed inside its bony structure. Her head hunched forward over her chest from age. She sat praying silently to herself. A routine she probably does often.

"Excuse me." I said as I sat down. "I think I have seen you here before. I was hoping I could ask you a few questions."

She finished her prayer, then looked in my direction and said. "Hello my child." She said as she gently tapped my knee. "I would be happy to answer your questions if I can."

"My name is Maria Alatorre and I am looking for a friend. We were here last week and I think you may have been here too. I was hoping you might know her and maybe where I could find her. Her name is Esmeralda Garcia." I proceeded to show her the picture, pointing out Esmeralda. She took the picture out of my hand and looked at it with squinty eyes, and immense curiosity.

"I do not know her but I know Javier Alatorre. Destructor de familias!" She said as she raised her fist in anger, denouncing him.

"I'm sorry, why would you say that?"

She lifted up the photograph and pointed at me. "This is not you. I know Maria and Javier Alatorre. Everyone in this neighborhood knows who they are. They destroyed my family and many others. You may look like her but your essence, your demeanor, and your attitude say otherwise."

I grabbed the picture out of her hand in disgust and dismay. I stood up and started to walk away while saying, "Thank you for your time."

As I stepped out into the aisle from the pew, the old woman asked a question.

"Tattoo, do you have the tattoo on your stomach?"

I stopped walking while I listened to her speak, never turning around to look at her. I only paused for a few seconds to hear her words. I knew the answer.

I was too rattled to drive so I decided to walk to the beach which was not close but was within walking distance. I needed to be by myself and think. I decided I was going to take the chance of not making it home before Javier.

When I got to the beach, the wind picked up. I could smell the wet salt in the air. I removed my sandals and walked to the water. Just feeling the water and sand between my toes was relaxing in itself but I took a short walk towards the pier where a few of the locals were fishing. As I approached the pier, a handful of kids were playing in the sand, making castles and digging water ways for the ocean to infiltrate the moat surrounding their castles. Their parents watching carefully. Under the pier, groups of teenagers were talking, drinking and smoking, with some, clearly needing privacy. Everyone's life seemed so normal, calm, no drama attached.

As I got close to the pier, I saw several benches up above so I walked towards the entrance. I wanted to sit down for a bit before I headed back. As I sat in silence I was recalling my conversation with the old lady from the church, the things that Esmeralda said to me before she left and the tattoo. Just then, I was startled by someone tapping me on my shoulder.

"Ma'am can you take a picture of us?" A strange woman asked.

"Of course." I said. I took her camera, let the couple pose in front of the water, and then snapped away.

"Thank you!" The two said in sync with each other. I smiled at them, handed the camera back and sat down once again. All of a sudden, I had a clear and powerful memory take over my body...

"Maia is everything on board?" Josh said loudly from the helm of the yacht.

"Yes, we are ready to sail!" I said, as I walked around to make sure we were completely untied. I was so excited. This was my first time visiting Mexico. I wanted to document everything so I went into my purse and grabbed my camera.

After walking around the boat to snap a few pictures, I made my way into the cabin to unpack a few things we would need for lunch. We sailed for about four hours, hugging the coastline just enough to barely see it, before Josh took a break to come in and eat lunch.

We talked about the cities we were planning on stopping at along the way, and how long we wanted to stay and what landmarks we wanted to explore. My voice was filled with excitement but Josh seemed preoccupied.

"What's wrong?" I asked with concern.

"Nothing. I'm just focused on getting there safely. We have some weather to deal with later."

"Well, you man the wheel and I will watch the radar. How about that!" I said, trying to cheer him up.

He got up from his seat while wiping off his face, leaned over the table towards me and planted a big kiss on my lips.

"Sounds like a good plan."

While Josh went back to driving the boat, I cleaned up our mess from lunch and then met up with him once again so I could keep him company and watch the weather.

We encountered some rough seas, wind and a small amount of rain, but we survived. Hopefully, that would be the worst weather we come across during our vacation.

The last city we were to visit was Mazatlán. I was determined to make the most out of our visit but Josh was not going to make it easy. He had been agitated all day. Walking around mumbling to himself, sometimes on the phone talking to someone who seemed to be making it worse. I figured it was work stuff and to be honest, I did not feel like hearing about it.

I went into our bedroom to pack a backpack for our excursion when I heard the boat engine cut off. Wondering why we were stopping, I dropped the bag onto the bed and looked out of one of the windows. I couldn't see Josh so I walked out of the bedroom and into the living room cabin to look for him.

Out of nowhere, a man grabbed me from behind as he placed a white cloth over my mouth. I instinctively grabbed the man's arm, trying to escape his power, wiggling back and forth with my body trying to get leverage somehow. I could smell something sweet as I attempted to breathe in fresh air through the piece of cloth, knowing it was the wrong thing to do. I could feel my body getting weaker and weaker. The man gently turned me around while trying to keep me on my feet the best he could.

"I'm sorry! I'm sorry! I don't know what else to do!"

"Why? I don't understand Josh!"

I looked around in a daze, feeling confused and desperate, with my legs starting to feel weak. Unable to hold my body up anymore, I fell into the chair next to me. Opening my eyes, closing my eyes, feeling the heaviness of them while trying to watch what was taking place.

I could hear a boat approaching ours. As the motor noise got louder and louder, Josh walked over to the side of our yacht to help them tie up. A scruffy-looking man boarded our boat, looked over at me, and then handed a duffle bag to my husband. Two other men, who were also standing on the boat deck, dropped four more bags next to his feet.

"There's the money that was agreed upon." The scruffy man said with a thick accent.

He walked towards me pulling something out of his pants pocket. I could hardly tell what was going on anymore. I was barely conscious. But before I completely passed out, I could feel a prick in my arm. He injected me with something.

His two sidekicks then took over, picking me up and taking me to their boat. Josh just stood there, rubbing his forehead, doing his best not to watch while I was taken away. The boat with me aboard drove off into the distance, getting smaller and smaller against the horizon. The last thing I remember seeing was our boat's name, Delicate Flower.

Josh couldn't move. He was paralyzed by what he had just done.

"I'm sorry Maia. I'm so sorry." He said softly into the blowing wind that was not listening.

The sound of a young girl screaming from catching her first fish woke me up from a very vivid flashback. I looked at my watch and realized it was a lot later than I had planned on leaving. I hurried to my car as fast as I could, trying to come up with a believable story while I drove home.

CHAPTER 13

"EVIDENCE"

As I got closer to the house, I started to get a nervous feeling in my stomach. It was getting dark outside which meant Javier was probably home. I turned onto the road that led up to our house when out of nowhere a beat up, old style van zoomed past me honking its horn. I slammed on my brakes just in time to watch it go by. I glanced into the window to see who was driving but the windows were tinted too dark for me to see inside. I continued to drive but the image of that van kept flashing in my mind because I lived in an upscale community, and those types of cars were not seen in this area.

I pulled into our long driveway, clicked the garage door opener so I could pull in and noticed that Javier's car was not there, nor were there any lights on that I could see. I must have beat him home. After closing the garage door, I walked inside, going from room to room calling out Javie's name but there was no response. This couldn't have worked out any better for me.

It was a beautiful night and since I was alone, I poured a glass of wine and went out to sit on the veranda in silence to think. I was feeling very alone and apprehensive. I had no family to help me and then the only woman I thought I could rely on was gone. My instincts were telling me not to trust Ava either. That photograph she gave me said it all.

In the months after I woke up from the coma, I felt like I had a fulfilled and rewarding life based on other people's stories, but the moment I stopped taking the medicine given to me by Dr. Ruiz, my life became clearer.

I took a drink of my wine and sighed, laying my head back against the pillow on the lounge chair I was sitting in. I was becoming mentally exhausted thinking about all this. The wine and the day's activities started to wear on me. I was feeling tired so I closed my eyes to rest…

The boat with me aboard drove off into the distance, getting smaller and smaller against the horizon. The last thing I remember seeing was our boats name, Delicate Flower.

As the drug began to wear off, I started to wake up but I was still too weak to open my eyes. Nevertheless, I could hear voices faintly talking to each other.

"How do you know what dosage is going to work?" Someone said.

"I have a good starting point but you know that this is experimental so you have to be prepared if it does not work."

"You're right doc. I just miss Maria so much." He said in a desperate voice.

I could hear feet shuffling on the ground. The sound was getting louder and louder. I could feel a warm body next to mine as I laid on what felt like a bed. Something soft and cold was being rubbed on my upper arm, then quickly a needle poked me. I was being injected with something again but I could not move to save myself, screaming within but my voice could not be heard. Once again, I slowly drifted off into sleep, sleeping for what seemed like an eternity.

"Maria, it's Javier, can you hear me.......wake up my love!"

Javier's face lit up with excitement as he fell down to one knee at the side of the bed. I slowly started to move my legs, then my arms, then I opened my eyes.

"I can't believe it. My beautiful wife has come back to me!" His eyes expressing happiness as he leaned over to kiss me on the cheek, then my forehead. Leaning into my body as close as he could get, trying to hug me a little hug.

I was awoken by a feeling of weightlessness. It was Javier picking me from the lounge chair. I didn't know how to react considering my feelings at that time, so I just grabbed him around the neck and held on until we reached the bed. I was not sure of my plans on how to confront him about his possible secrets. Honestly, at that point, I was not in the correct state of mind. In fact, I acted like I was still half asleep when we reached the bedroom, rolling over onto my side after he set me down. He didn't say anything to me either. He went into the bathroom turning on the shower. By the time he got into bed I had already dozed off.

The next morning I realized that I never put back the picture I took of Esmeralda. I'm sure Javier wouldn't notice such a small thing but I did not want to take a chance. When I went into the kitchen to look for Javier, I did not see him so I quickly walked into the living room and put the photo back.

I was hungry so I started to make breakfast, figuring Javier would show up sooner or later. After about ten minutes, I could hear two men talking. It was Javier and Mateo coming up from the lower level.

"Something sure does smell delicious!" Mateo said.

The two men walked into the kitchen area, where I was standing by the oven cooking eggs. Javier walked over to give me a morning kiss on the cheek. I was trying not to look at them, looking Javier in the eye would be difficult because of the "secrets" I had just uncovered.

"Where did you two just come from?" I said with curiosity.

"Mateo's working on a project for me so I had to show him where he can store some of the products we're shipping." Javier said quickly. "We're heading off to work now."

Mateo and Javier walked towards the front door, trying to avoid any more of my questions.

I followed behind asking them, "I'm not busy, maybe I can help you out today?"

Javier opened the door for Mateo to walk through. Turning around to look at me while standing in the doorway he said, "I appreciate you offering Maria but I have plenty of men to help out. I'll see you tonight. Let's go out to dinner. We haven't spent much time together lately so let me make it up to you. Pick out a restaurant for us to go to."

Javier walked out, shutting the door behind him while I stood there for a moment with my hands crossed in front of my chest, trying to hold back the resentment that was starting to build up.

I went back to eating my breakfast for now. Later in the afternoon, I went to Javier's office hoping that he had forgotten to lock the door. Unfortunately, luck was not on my side. I had nothing else to do so I went back into the kitchen, opened the bottom drawer of the built-in desk, and grabbed the telephone book so I could look up a restaurant for the night.

Sitting down at the kitchen island, I skimmed through the restaurant advertisements, finally choosing one. I called a restaurant to make a reservation, choosing a time later in the evening as I knew that Javier wouldn't be home early. As I talked to the person on the phone, I attempted to close the phone book at the same time but it didn't close all the way. It opened a page for local libraries. An advertisement on the top of the page caught my eye, it said they had computers that were free for the community to use. I got excited to see this, so I finished my conversation on the phone and made my way to the library location listed in the ad.

Pulling into the parking lot, I noticed that there were a lot of cars. I found myself praying that there were computers available to use. I walked inside and looked around, noticing most of the people were sitting at tables with open books and notepads in front of them but I did not see the computers. I walked up to the library's main desk and asked a short, older lady for help.

"Hello ma'am. Is there someone here who can show me how to use one of your computers? I don't know much about them." I said.

"Yes. I have a nice young man who can help you. Why don't you go into the computer room over there, pick out one and I will send him to you."

"Thank you."

I walked to the room she pointed to. Luckily, there were several open computers. I chose the one in the corner that felt more private. I didn't have to wait too long before the teenage boy showed up.

"Hi, my name is Luis. I was told you're not very familiar with computers."

"No, I'm not." I said in embarrassment.

He pulled up a chair next to me, showing me step by step of what to do and how to research information using the internet. He was so patient that I felt very at ease asking him questions that only a child would ask. After about thirty minutes or so, he asked if I had felt comfortable enough to use the computer by myself. I told him I would try because the truth is that, I did not want him to know what I was researching.

After he left, I started typing Javier's first and last name into the web browser. On the top of the page were pictures of Javier, some head shots for his company and some that looked like snapshots of him walking around town. Below the images were a few articles about his company. Then towards the end of the page, I saw a tag line about an investigation into his business and possible criminal activities; human trafficking to be exact.

I clicked on the article to read it. The page however had an error message instead of an article. *What is happening?* I thought. I clicked the back arrow to try again, but the same error message showed up.

I went back again to the main page to see if other articles worked. All of the web results about his company opened but this one article. I decide to do another search of Javier's name and human trafficking together. The page loaded with a few more articles from news websites but those links did not work either.

I became frustrated and upset. I decided to type in one more scenario. *Maria Alatorre car accident.* Nothing! If Javier was so well known in this area why would my car accident not be in the news? A prominent business man whose wife almost died did not make the news?

Before I left, I found Luis and thanked him for his help. Driving home, I decided that at dinner, I was going to push Javier and ask him questions. I had to be careful, I thought, because he had no idea that I had stopped taking those memory suppressing pills.

As the evening approached, I started to get ready for our dinner date. I took a long, hot shower while conjuring up my plans to confront Javier. I wanted to get more details about my car accident, why Esmeralda left and about his work. After all, wouldn't these be normal questions a wife would ask her husband, especially considering the fact I am supposed to have amnesia.

I got out of the shower, dried myself off and wrapped a towel around my body so I could walk into my closet to pick out an outfit. As I was going through my clothes, my cell phone rang. I walked back into the bathroom where my phone was sitting by the sink and I could see on the screen that it was Javier. I picked up the phone to answer it while sighing inside because I had a bad feeling about what he was about to say.

"Hello." I said.

"Maria I have bad news." Javier said in a sad tone. "I have a problem at work that I need to attend to. I have to cancel our date tonight."

"Javier you promised!"

"I know but this is an emergency. I wouldn't cancel on you if it wasn't."

"You haven't been around. Esmeralda is gone. I am lonely. I have nothing to do in this big house."

"Why don't I send Ava over to keep you company tonight?" He said trying to come up with something to keep me satisfied.

"No Javie. I am not in the mood to be around anyone else. I was planning on talking to my husband all night."

"I know. I know."

"You definitely need to make this up to me and soon." I demanded.

"I will my love." Javier hung up the phone. After that conversation, I realized that I really didn't have anyone in my life to talk to.

I finished getting dressed and put on my clog slippers so I could safely walk around the house. I twisted my long, black wet hair into a bun on top of my head, holding it down with a hair clip. After all, there was no point in spending the time drying it. I had nowhere to go.

I walked down the hallway and into the living room. The wall of windows allowed the brightness of the moonlight to illuminate the back side of the house, just enough to see where to place my footsteps. I didn't turn on any lights. The mood of the house matched my mood. I went into the kitchen to make a cappuccino and to grab a small snack. I was no longer in the right state of mind to eat a big meal.

I wanted to be comfortable, so I sat on the couch, close to the living room windows. It had big, oversized pillows along the back, soft and cozy. I sat down, leaning my left side against the pillows, and looking out over the back of the couch, into the dark, vast ocean. It was hard to distinguish where the ocean ended and where the star-filled sky began. It was mesmerizing to say the least.

As I sat on the couch, I must have fallen asleep because I woke up to a faint noise coming from the lower level. I slowly sat up on the edge of the couch, patiently listening to make sure that I did hear a noise. Yes! I heard it! I got up and made my way down the steps, softly touching the railing to guide me. I stopped at the bottom to listen again. This time, the muffled noise sounded like voices. I perked up when I realized where it was coming from; the hidden hallway.

It was dark so I could barely see. My left hand maintaining contact with the wall so I could find my way. I stumbled into the cold room with the moving bookcase. This room was even darker, tucked away in the back of the basement it had no light sources. I remembered however that most of the small tables with the chairs on both sides had cigars, cigarette trays and matches. Touching everything as I walked, having no luck getting my eyes to adapt to the darkness, I finally found one of the tables. Fumbling around with my fingers, I successfully found a book of matches.

I struck one of the matches which lit up the room just enough to see directly in front of me. The first match ran out quickly, slightly burning the tips of my fingers as it faded out. I dropped it on the table and struck another one. This time I walked to the bookcase to search for the book that triggered its opening. It took me several times but at last I triumphed over this adversity. I felt the bookcase jolt a little; the sign that it had unlocked and opened.

I stretched my hand towards the light that was shining through the gap, slowly opening it just enough to peak my head inside to see what was going on.

Farther down the hallway, close to one of the hanging lights on the wall, were three girls whispering to each other by one of the cell doors. Peeking though the cell bars on the other side was another girl. Her fingers wrapped around the bars so tight, her knuckles were devoid of flowing blood. I quietly made my way in their direction. As I got closer, I could hear loud footsteps echoing from the darkness of the hallway. Getting louder and louder as the noise got closer. The person entered into the lit area and I could see it was Esmeralda. I started jogging this time, feeling safe enough to open my mouth.

"Esmeralda!" I yelled just loud enough for all of them to hear me. All of the girls screamed in response to my calling out. I could hear Esmeralda telling the girls to be quiet and calm down. She made her way past the girls and whispered; "Mrs. Alatorre?"

"What is going on?!" I could feel my heart fluttering from the excitement of the situation.

"No time Mrs. Alatorre!" She turned toward the cell with a tool to cut off the lock, letting the caged girl out. She then turned back towards me and said. "I need you to trust me. I need you to come with me!"

I stood there dumbfounded, watching her go from cell to cell, cutting off the locks to let more girls out. Esmeralda kept yelling at the girls to run, that she would let the other girls free. A few of them were stumbling and falling while trying to move their legs fast enough to escape.

"Let me help." I walked up to her as she unlocked yet another door.

"They are all out. Mrs. Alatorre, how did you get in here?"

"That secret door." I pointed down the hall. Esmeralda could barely see it.

"Go close it. Quickly!" I ran down the hall to shut the door but before I did I stood in front of the door for a second and thought to myself. *Once I shut this door and go with Esmeralda, Javier will know that my amnesia was gone, that I have woken up from a drug injected nightmare thrust upon me by Dr. Ruiz and himself. He would know whose side I was on.*

Click! I shut the door. Running towards Esmeralda felt like I was running towards freedom. At that moment, I knew I had made the right choice. As I reached her, she grabbed my hand and led the way down the dark corridor, with our bodies illuminating each time we passed one of the string lights. It felt like we ran for a mile.

We exited the hidden tunnel and got into the car that Esmeralda was driving. All the girls were gone, some ran into the woods, while others ran along the beach, but they were all free because of Esmeralda.

At first, we sat in silence as she drove the car like a professional race car driver. Maneuvering past slower cars, paying no attention to them honking at her, never letting up out of fear of being followed. Holding onto my seatbelt and the door's arm rest, I glanced in the direction of Esmeralda not only noticing the deep determination on her face, but also noticing the sadness.

CHAPTER 14

"Where did you get this car and how did you know about those girls?" I asked.

"It's a friend's. Someone I am staying with."

"And the girls?"

"I have been following Javier's men."

"Esmeralda?" I paused for a moment. "Javier's a human trafficker, isn't he?"

"Yes." She said while trying to concentrate on driving.

"Why didn't you tell me? I trusted you!"

"Maria, Javier is a very bad man. People fear him. He has ruined many lives in our town. If you stand up to him, well, let's just say you usually are never seen again."

"So why now? Why are you standing up to him now and helping me?" I said with anger in my voice.

"He took Lucy!" Esmeralda started crying which made me start to cry. I then knew her desperation. Her only daughter had been taken from her. Any mother would sacrifice her life to save her own child's. This just reassured me that leaving with her was the right thing to do.

Instead of talking, I reached over to touch Esmeralda's hand. I wanted her to know that I was on her side and even though I felt betrayed by her, I forgave her.

We must have drove two hours through the countryside that evening, passing a few small villages in the middle of nowhere, transitioning from open land to wooded forests, with the moon shining bright, illuminating the tips of the oak and pine trees. Seeing the beauty of this world is breathtaking, but on the other hand, knowing the evil in this world is disheartening.

Esmeralda started to slow the car down in anticipation of making a turn. I perked up in my seat to see where we were going. A small, glowing lantern attached to a rustic post appeared on the side of the road, signaling for her to make the turn. The gravel road was dark, bumpy and covered with a canopy of trees. Only the headlights of the car made the road visible to the eye. Behind us was a trail of dust that disappeared almost instantly into the night. I looked around attentively, trying to remember any landmarks we past just in case I was ever on my own.

Suddenly, the claustrophobic feel of the wooded road opened up to a meadow area, exposing the roadway leading to an old-fashioned covered bridge. It looked unstable and crossed over a raging river below. It definitely wasn't inviting to say the least.

"Esmeralda stop!" I screamed in fear.

Hearing the panic in my voice, she pressed on the brakes to stop the car.

"What's wrong?" She asked.

"Are we going over that bridge?" I pointed, while looking at her at the same time with an expression on my face that could be only described as terrified.

"It'll be ok. The darkness makes it look spooky. I've been over it many times and it's as sturdy as a rock."

The car started moving forward, entering the mouth of the bridge. Hearing my nervous moans, Esmeralda maintained a slow, steady pace so I didn't become more spooked.

The moon rays penetrated each window opening along the bridge as we drove through. Creaks and cracks grumbling below the tires didn't make me feel better. Suddenly, the car jolted because of the bumpy transition from the bridge to the gravel road. I felt embarrassed that I acted like that. Owing to the fact that my mind was clear from drugs, I felt like I was starting to learn a lot more about myself.

Just over the bridge was our final destination. Esmeralda parked the car on the left side of a house, placing me closer to the front door. The Adobe style house was lit up by a single light near the front porch that had no cover on it. The house was painted a rustic red color and had a chimney sprouting from the center of the home. It had a yard that was a mix of powdery dirt and sprouts of grass. Pieces of wrought iron artwork hung sporadically on the outside walls for decoration.

We both got out of the car at the same time, but I waited by my door until Esmeralda came around. She waved at me to follow her inside. When we entered the home, a very old man with a bald head and long white beard was sitting in a chair sleeping while a cigar was burning itself out in an ash tray next to him.

"That's Maximo Mendez. He's an old family friend who is allowing me to stay here while I look for Lucy." Esmeralda explained as she walked over to put his cigar out.

"Maximo. Maximo wake up." She pushed the old man on his shoulder several times.

"Huh? What? Who's there?"

"Maximo, it's Esmeralda. I'm back. I brought my friend Maria with me too. You need to go to bed."

"Oh, okay." He said as he got out of his comfortable chair, waved at me, and then walked out of the room.

Esmeralda turned on a light so we could see better. The room was filled with old style furniture and traditional Mexican covers thrown over most of them. Brightly colored paintings hung on most of the walls. The inside matched the outside.

"I know you have a lot of questions Maria." She said as she walked towards me. "I promise to tell you everything."

"You were right about the pills." I proclaimed. "I stopped taking them." She wrapped her arms around me and gave me a tight hug.

Talking into her ear I said, "You saved those girls and now I will help you find Lucy."

Whispering in my ear, her soft, motherly voice uttered, "We will talk tomorrow about everything."

"Promise?" I said while hugging her back.

"Promise."

Esmeralda showed me to an empty bedroom where I could sleep. Opening the closet door in the room, she showed me clothes that used to belong to Maximo's wife, telling me that we are about the same size and that these were all the clothes she had.

I rolled around in bed the entire night. My mind was wandering about the past, the future and everything in between. I was full of anxiety because of what Esmeralda was going to tell me but eventually, the exhaustion from the day's events took over and I fell asleep.

I woke up to the clinking and banging of pots and pans. It sounded like someone was in the kitchen making breakfast. After getting out of bed, I got myself dressed and looked out the window to see what I had missed the night before. The sky was overcast today. A few yards away, there was a thick forest with a dirt walking path entering a jungle of trees. An old barn was positioned by the side of the house where a few goats and chickens were roaming around the outskirts of the building. It looked like we were on a small farm, completely in solitude.

I walked through the house looking at all the artwork on the walls as I tried to find the kitchen. The house was filled with paintings. I wondered if Maximo was the artist. He looked like an artist. Each painting was more interesting than the last. A compilation of realism and abstract styles; very unique.

I was clearly getting closer to the kitchen based on the aroma of the food getting stronger and stronger. As I entered, I saw Maximo drinking a cup of coffee at a small table next to a sliding glass door. Esmeralda was at the stove cooking, a sight I missed markedly.

"Good morning Maria. Are you hungry?" Esmeralda inquired.

"Yes. Thank you."

"Sit down. I'll bring you some coffee."

I walked over to the table, and nodded a hello to Maximo. I must admit I felt a little uncomfortable. He nodded hello back to me and said, "I hope your accommodations were acceptable."

"Of course they were. I appreciate you opening your home to me." At that point, Esmeralda put a hot cup of coffee in front of me, with the steam billowing outward clearly indicating it was too hot to drink just yet.

"The paintings on the walls, are they yours Maximo?" I asked, trying to start a conversation.

"They are my late wife's handy work. She was pretty well known back in the day. I lost her ten years ago."

"I am so sorry for your loss. They are very good. I can see why she was popular." I picked up my coffee to take a test sip.

"After she passed, I decided to hang all the ones we had left. It helps keep her in my thoughts as I get older." His eyes were very expressive. You could see that he was upset about getting older, probably forgetting her little by little in his old age.

Esmeralda eventually joined us at the table, bringing a plate of food for each of us. We sat talking while we ate but the whole time, I was asking myself, "*When are Esmeralda and I going to talk?*"

Maximo got up from the table first. He said he was going out to the barn to feed the animals. Esmeralda got up next, taking both of our empty plates with her. When she got to the sink to clean the dishes she said, "I know you're wondering when we are going to talk. I was hoping we could take a walk. I know a nice quiet place."

"Sure, that sounds good." I said, while finishing my coffee.

The dishes were done. The kitchen was clean. The early morning transitioned into late morning. At that instant, our walk was inevitable.

I was standing outside, in front of the house watching Maximo from afar. I could tell he was a man who hardly sat down, a man who kept busy for the sake of his sanity. I was totally astonished by the stamina he embodied.

I heard the front door open, it was Esmeralda ready to go on our stroll. We walked together down the dirt path making small talk, mostly about when I first woke up from my coma. It only took a few minutes to get to an opening that overlooked the river gorge that we had driven across the night before. It was stunningly beautiful. I walked closer to the edge to take a look. The gorge was fairly shallow in this area. It was easy to see the rushing, clear water hammering the rocks scattered throughout the river. There were a few trees crossing the water that had fallen over, allowing animals to traverse it easily. A cold mist rose up every so often to penetrate my face and send a slight chill up my body. The setting was definitely cooler than where I lived by the beach.

"Maria come sit down." Esmeralda said as she patted the top of a bench that was made out of logs. I closed my eyes for a few seconds and took a deep breath so I could try to get that nervous feeling out of my stomach before

Esmeralda told me my real life story. I walked over to her, sat down and looked into her eyes. I could see that she was nervous too.

"First, I want to apologize for leaving the way I did. I had to because of Lucy." She uttered in a soft, comforting tone.

"I understand."

"Are you honestly ready to hear the truth? I suspect it will change your opinion about Javier and it may change your opinion about me because I am not going to hold anything back. If we can have a relationship in the future, I want it to be honest from this point on."

Once again I took a deep breath and said, "Yes."

"You said you have been having dreams, tell me about them."

"It's the same dream over and over but each one becomes more detailed than the last. I am on a yacht with a man, he ends up drugging me. A couple of other men board the yacht. They give the man I was with black bags of what I can only assume is money because I end up being taken away onto another boat. Like they were doing a business exchange."

"Let me start from the beginning and eventually that dream will make sense." Esmeralda said as she patted the top one of my hands as if to say everything will be okay.

"Mr. Alatorre was devastated to hear that his wife had been in a car accident. Maria was the love of his life. They did everything together. She was even involved in his trafficking business."

"Wait." I interrupted her. "You're talking about me right? I mean you're saying things in the past tense."

"His wife died that night," she paused for a brief second. "You are not Maria Alatorre. Your real name is Maia Carson. You are Maria's twin sister."

"What! That can't be true!" I screamed.

She continued, "Neither of you knew about the other. Mr. Alatorre found you by accident because he ended up meeting your real husband Josh Carson through a business acquaintance of his."

"Those are the two names from my dream. I remember now. I called him Josh and he called me Maia. I can't believe this. It wasn't a dream, it was a memory?"

"Yes. When Mr. Alatorre found out that you existed he came up with a plan, along with Dr. Ruiz, to have you replace Maria. Since you were her twin, I'm guessing he assumed you two would be exactly like each other. He was never the same after her death. He completely changed. In a very short amount of time it affected his business, his friendships, everything. Knowing you were out there created a new passion in him. I think by having you around, he thought it would help him mourn but at the same time he would attempt to mold you into Maria."

"They wanted to manipulate me with the drugs?" I asked.

"Javier and Dr. Ruiz have been experimenting on a new drug that would suppress memories. It was something Dr. Ruiz had been working on for a while. He finally figured it out. Dr. Ruiz is not a good man either. They didn't know if it would truly work so when you woke up and he saw that it had worked, Mr. Alatorre was the happiest he had been since Maria's death. He was secretly telling Dr. Ruiz how you were acting; he made sure to alert him if you were saying anything related to your past life, or anything that would let the doctor know that the drug was wearing off."

"And if it wasn't for you telling me to stop those pills, I may not be here right now."

"I don't know, possibly."

"What if it didn't work? What were they going to do with me?" I solicited.

"I don't know Maia."

"Maia?" I said. "It sounds weird that you just called me that."

"Well, that is who you are."

"I suppose." As I said that, I realized that Esmeralda was not innocent. She conspired with them for a while. "You're acting like you care now but why would you agree to help out with his plan. I was preyed upon by Javier and you knew that he was going to ruin my life!"

"Lucy," she said simply. "I promised myself that I would do anything to keep Lucy away from him, to keep my head down."

I didn't know what to say to that. I was trying not to overreact because most mothers would do anything to protect their children. I did not live in her shoes.

"Maia, I know that I do not deserve your forgiveness. What I did was horrible but I need you to know that I was a single mother with a baby and Mr. Alatorre gave me a job that I was lucky to have. I had to ignore a lot of things to survive. At first, I stayed for the paycheck to support my daughter, then when I found out about his trafficking business so I stayed out of fear for our lives. He is known for murdering people who do not abide by his rules and as Lucy got older, I stayed out of fear he would traffic her. I felt that if I kept working for him I would have an advantage. I was able to hide her from him but unfortunately, she made the mistake of coming to your house. I knew then that I had to make a decision and so I decided that I would try to hide Lucy and tell you the truth. But I guess I really didn't save anyone in the end."

Does she deserve forgiveness? I don't know. At the time, I could only remember bits and pieces of how I got to that point and how she helped me escaped Javier's grip. All I could hope for was that the drugs Dr. Ruiz gave me hadn't affected all my memories.

"So you're telling me that my real husband sold me to Javier." I was hoping her answer would be no.

"I don't think Josh is a human trafficker. I don't know the details but I think your husband was desperate for money for some reason, so Mr. Alatorre made him an offer."

"And Josh took it." I said as I put my hands over my face and started to cry. I couldn't take it anymore. I got up to take a break from the insanity; it was too much to take in. Standing by the edge of the gorge, my mind was filled with so many questions. Visions of that day on the boat took over, then visions of my short life with Javier. My feelings were ranging from sadness to confusion and then anger. Hearing the harsh crashing of the water over the rocks below just intensified my feelings at that moment.

I heard Esmeralda stand up and walk over to me. When she reached me, she stood by my side, a little behind me and placed her right hand on my shoulder.

"It's going to be okay Maia."

"Tell me about my sister."

"Obviously, she was a beautiful woman like you but it is now clear that both of you were brought up in two different worlds. She was a ruthless woman when it came to their trafficking business but at home with me, she had her moments of compassion, though not many. She had the same attitude as Mr. Alatorre. They are arrogant, greedy, and callous. She didn't talk to me the way you do. She saw me as the servant and not as a friend, so it was nice when you treated me differently."

"The truth is, you treated me with kindness from the beginning and you didn't have to confess to me here or even help me understand what was going on." I was trying to compliment her honesty.

Esmeralda walked back to the bench to sit down and I followed behind her. This conversation was taking a lot out of the both of us. We needed to rest not only our bodies but our minds.

"This is hard for both of us in different ways and I appreciate your efforts. I really do." I admitted to her.

"You saying that to me shows the difference between Maria and yourself. You have a caring soul."

"Thanks."

I think we both needed a break so we decided to walk back to the house to help Maximo finish his daily chores. Walking up to the barn, we found the poor man hunched over, scooping up hay with a pitch fork to feed the goats and horses. I quickly marched over to assume the task and told him to take a break while Esmeralda milked one of the cows that was resting in one of the larger horse stalls. As we were finishing up, the sun was directly above our heads, indicating it was almost lunch time. Esmeralda suggested we all cleaned up by taking showers before sitting down to eat. We all happily agreed to that.

Maximo and Esmeralda beat me to the kitchen. I was kind of disappointed because I wanted to help with the cooking this time. Sometimes, I felt like I was being catered to, and that I needed to pull my weight.

Maximo was cutting up vegetables at the kitchen table. Esmeralda was cooking fish in a pan while scrambling to get out another pan from the cabinet below.

"Wow it smells great in here!" I exclaimed.

"Fish tacos. Esmeralda makes the best fish tacos." Maximo told me as he finished cutting the ingredients for the pico de gallo.

"What can I do to help?" I asked.

"It's a beautiful afternoon. Why don't you go wipe down the table on the patio so we can sit outside and set the table with the plates and utensils?" Esmeralda suggested with a happy tone in her voice. She, like myself, probably felt like a weight had been lifted off her shoulders, like the tension had dissipated temporarily.

"I would be happy to." I said, as I watched Maximo slowly walk to the refrigerator while Esmeralda finished cooking.

I finished cleaning the table just in time. Esmeralda brought out the food on a platter so we could assemble our own tacos. Maximo grabbed a bottle of beer for each of us while I went inside to grab the plates and utensils.

It was nice sitting around a table talking and eating. Usually, I was always alone because Javier was never home. We started to talk about Lucy. Esmeralda said she had an idea of where she could be. Apparently, after Lucy was taken, she spent all of her time watching Javier and his men. She had been following them, talking to locals, learning where they house the girls and exchange them with their buyers.

"Is that how you knew those girls were at my house?" I asked Esmeralda.

"It was. I never knew those cells were there the entire time I worked for Mr. Alatorre. You surprised me when you showed up Maia." Again the Maia, it sounded really odd.

Maximo interjected, "He is a dangerous man. You better make sure you're ready for this fight."

"I'm helping you. We have a better chance of getting her back with the both of us working together." I said without hesitation.

"Are you sure? I don't know how Mr. Alatorre will react when he finds out you are helping me. You can just walk away now. You can stay here with Maximo. He has connections. We can figure out how to get you back to the United States."

What she said really hit me hard. I had been through a nightmare. I could easily save myself, find a new place to live and start over.

"No. No I am helping you find your daughter." Esmeralda picked up her beer bottle, held it up in the air over the center of the table. Maximo and I reached for ours too, raised them up high in the center of the table, clinking them all together all at once in unity.

CHAPTER 15

Business has not gone smoothly for Javier lately. He had been able to find enough girls to traffic but they had not been up to his standards so it took up a lot of his time, Javier and his men were discussing business at their favorite bar; drinking, smoking and eating. A few locals were also entertaining themselves but kept their distance from Javier and his men. Most of the locals won't even look at Javier or his men in the eye, knowing the possible consequences if their facial expressions were taken in an offensive or threatening way.

"What happened to the last shipment Glitch?" Javier wanted answers.

"I was told that the cargo ship we used got boarded by Pirates from Southeast Asia."

"This was no coincidence." Javier said. "They took our girls, so they were tipped off by someone."

"Definitely." Glitch said while taking a drag off his cigarette.

"I want the snitch found and taken care of."

"Raul and I will take care of it Boss."

"Good."

Javier and his men continued to talk about the next shipment of girls; the girls that were being held at his house.

"We have a new buyer in France. I spoke to him earlier today and everything is set up. Our Moldova contact will help transfer them through Europe." Javier explained as he took a few bites of his food. "We are expanding our clientele gentlemen, so this first set of girls need to get there without any complications."

Raul butted in. "Boss, it's getting harder and harder to find girls. I think we need to talk about where to look next."

"Yes, this is becoming a problem." Javier mumbled.

"We need to start looking in Puerta Vallarta." Raul chimed in. "I have cousins there that are always raving about the beautiful women. Tourists too. We could expand our options by trafficking women from other countries."

"That's a possibility Raul. I like it. I like it." A clear smirk rose on Javier's face as he responded.

Just then Javier's cell phone rang. It was Oscar, one of his new hires that was sent over to Javier's house to feed and check on the girls. He was a younger man in his mid-twenties that had proven his loyalty to Javier and the business in recent years.

"Mr. Alatorre, the girls are gone!" He talked so loudly and emphatically that Javier almost didn't understand what he was saying.

"They're gone? What do you mean they're gone?"

"When I pulled up to the door, it was open. It looks like someone cut the lock. I went inside and all the girls are gone."

Javier covered his phone and told his men to move out and head to his house. The girls were gone.

"And be quiet! Maria is at home!"

Javier started to talk to Oscar again while he got up from the booth and headed out. Glitch and Raul followed right behind him.

"Oscar we are on our way. Stay there." Javier got into the backseat of the SUV with Glitch driving and Raul in the passenger seat. Glitch drove furiously, disregarding the speed limit and traffic signs. Maneuvering his way through the city streets and then the shoreline road along the beach to our house, he eventually caught up with the other men.

As the herd of cars got closer to the house, they turned off their lights and slowed down, passing our house on the left until they reached the door hidden by the grassy knoll.

Everyone jumped out of their cars, running towards Oscar, with some going inside and others congregating around him asking questions. Javier strolled through the door, looking around, taking in everything he saw. Walking down the hallway, he noticed all the locks had been cut off, some of the pieces broken indicating someone didn't know what they were doing. About halfway down, he stopped at one of the cells, looked inside it, and then back over his shoulder at his men.

"Oscar, come here."

"Yes Mr. Alatorre?"

"You didn't see or hear anything?"

"No Sir."

"Walk down to the end of the hallway, come back and tell me what you see."

The young man ran down the hallway until he came to a dead end. He looked around but it was very dark so he pulled out his cell phone from his back pocket and turned on his phone's camera light. Again, he carefully looked but saw nothing. He ran back to Mr. Alatorre as fast as he could, so he would not disappoint him.

The young man said, "I don't see anything Mr. Alatorre. Just a wall."

Javier didn't say anything to Oscar. He merely turned around and said, "Glitch, drive me to the house."

Javier and Glitch left the building while the other men hung around outside by the cars to wait for instructions.

Quietly driving up to the house, Javier got out of the car and told Glitch to wait for him. First walking into our bedroom to find an empty bed, then checking the bathroom. Very concerned, he walked over to the windows, looked out onto the veranda knowing that this was not a good sign. He stood there staring out the window, engulfed in his own thoughts for a few minutes.

Next, he went into his office to look at the surveillance videos on his computer but they were blank. Someone cut the feeds. Someone who knew there were security cameras.

Javier then went into the man cave to see if I had been down there. He noticed that one of the tables had been out of place and saw a book of matches on the ground that I had dropped when the secret door popped open. A lot of suspicions entered his mind.

Javier walked back upstairs to meet up with Glitch but decided to call my cell phone first. Standing in the foyer with his phone to his ear listening eagerly, hearing what sounded like an echo, he moved his phone down by his side next to his pant leg. He turned towards the living room where he saw my phone on the table next to the couch, lighting up and ringing. He was dumbfounded at the thought that I was probably gone. He was paralyzed at the idea of me finding the girls, letting them go and running away myself. Javier wasn't sure what to do. He thought about calling Dr. Ruiz just in case the pills were not working anymore but he quickly changed his mind. He decided to first figure out what was going on before he involved the doctor.

Javier walked back to the SUV, opened the door and got in. Leaning his head back onto the headrest, he informed Glitch that I was not in the house.

"Glitch, you are my most loyal and trustworthy employee. There are only a few people I can trust right now. I need you to find Maria. Get in touch with Mateo and Ava for help. I will tell Raul to find out what happened to the missing girls. Keep this between you and me. I want to find out if she is involved first."

"Do you really think it was her?"

"She may have found them and panicked. She has not been the same person since the accident, and it doesn't help that I have not been at home with her." Javier said as he gestured with his hand to drive back to the other men.

One of the henchmen standing outside by the door to the hallway signaled for the other men to gather around as he saw the SUV coming back. As the large vehicle stopped on the gravel road, the dust from the rocks pillowed upward, causing the air to thicken with dirt. The light beams from the car only enhanced the visibility of the powdery particles.

Javier got out to speak to his men. "Raul...I am putting you in charge of finding the girls. Grab some men and start searching now. No one is to stop looking until I say so. Glitch is going to be with me. I need a few of you to stay back and watch my house and this entrance." Javier turned and walked away to make a phone call. Glitch continued to talk to the men about where to start.

Standing by the side of his SUV for privacy, Javier dialed Mateo.

"Hello."

"Mateo, I have a problem. Someone released the girls that were supposed to be shipped in a few days. Worse than that, Maria is gone. I think it may have been her."

"Do you think the pills stopped working?"

"More than likely. I think she found the hidden door to the cells. Glitch is the only one who knows. I told him to contact you and Ava for help so he will be calling soon. He still doesn't know about Maria so you need to be careful."

"All right."

"Also, whoever did this cut the houses security camera wires so I have no video."

"I will contact Node to see if he can find anything." Mateo said. "I thought you put a chip in Maria when she was in the coma?"

"I changed my mind. I felt guilty." Javier paused for a moment. "I'll call you later."

All of Javier's crew knew their assigned jobs so they scattered throughout the town to investigate. The crew combed through the known hangouts for thugs, hooligans, riffraff and snitches; those who will do anything for money. They spent the night harassing local business owners, people walking the streets and even the homeless in hopes of getting any tips about the girls.

Finally, Raul came upon a few teenagers hanging at a small park by the beach just north of the house. Two boys were leaning up against a picnic table while a girl sat on top of it giggling at their every word.

"Hey! Have you guys seen anything unusual tonight?" Raul asked.

"Piérdete amigo!" One of the kids uttered as he stood up. Raul did not take kindly to his rude response so he grabbed the kid by the shirt, pushed him back to where he was laying flat on his back on top of the table, with one of his legs in the air to balance himself.

"Escuche aquí, pequeño punk. ¡No volveré a preguntar amablemente! ¿Habla usted Inglés?" Raul demanded.

"Yes, yes I speak English!" The boy feeling terrified by what he just got himself into.

Raul let the boy return to his feet as the other two kids remained where they were.

"Let's try this again. I am looking for some girls that may have come by here on foot, possibly asking for help. Have you seen them?"

The girl interjected quickly. "I saw two girls running along the beach. They looked like they were crying. Their clothes were all messed up, dirty."

"How long ago was this?"

"Maybe an hour."

"Did you notice anything else?"

"No, they just kept walking up the beach that way." She pointed north.

Raul and his men got into their car and headed in that direction. Raul called Javier on their way to let him know they had some information about the direction some of the girls were headed. Javier then called Mateo so his hacker friend, Node, could look in the area.

Node is the best hacker in town. He will do anything for anybody if the price is right but Javier was his main income source. Javier will pay top notch for quick and efficient results and Node never disappoints.

"Mateo it's Node! One of Mr. A's neighbors has security cameras that I was able to hack into. A car with two people inside drove away from his house that night. I was able to track them until they got into the countryside, North East of town. I will text you the coordinates."

"Good work. Let me know if you find anything else." Mateo hung up with Node. His phone chiming from a text alert with the coordinates. He immediately called Javier.

Javier and Glitch were at his house in the office contacting all the buyers of the girls that got away. Knowing that these recent incidents of not coming through with product would cause major problems with his network of clients, Javier offered incentives and discounts for the next shipments so his clients could make bigger profits off the girls. Just as he hung up with his last client, his phone rang. It was Mateo.

"Good news Javier. Node found a car that was on scene that night. He followed it as far as he could and sent me the last coordinates."

"Could he tell who was in the car?" Javier questioned.

"No. He could tell there were two people but that was it."

"All right. Call Raul and tell him to keep searching for the girls. Send me those coordinates. Glitch and I will search for that car. I have a feeling I know who it is."

"Do you need help? I can meet up with you."

"I'll call if I do. I need you to stay where you are. Keep working with Node." Javier instructed.

Glitch heard what Javier was saying so he went out to the SUV to get ready to move out while Javier finished his call. Mateo not only sent him the coordinates, but also a screenshot of the car. It was a beat up, older car that was a medium blue color with a hatchback. Luckily, the image was clear enough that perhaps they could use it to show other people.

The two men made their way out of town and into the vast countryside. When they got to the area that the car was last seen, they stopped at every house, business and gas station off the main road to ask questions. It was getting late so most of the businesses were closed for the day; businesses likely operated by people who also had households to run in the evenings. Most businesses in these small towns only stayed open for a part of the day.

They eventually came upon a gas station that was open. The two men went inside in hopes that they would get some answers. After all, they were running out of options on the main road and there were too many small, side roads. It would take forever to conquer all of them in one night.

It was a tiny gas station with two pumps. An older man was attending the tiny store inside. It had a counter for the register and two isles of miscellaneous stuff, just enough for the old man to make extra money.

When Javier and Glitch walked in, the old man stood up from his resting stool to say hello.

"Hola Amigos?" His old eyes squinting to see who was in his establishment.

Javier pulled out his phone to show him the picture of the car. "Have you seen this car today?"

The old man turned his body slightly to reach for his eye glasses on the counter next to him, put them on and said, "Sí, Sí."

"What can you tell me about the people in the car?"

"One of the señoras pumped gas, then came in to pay." Scratching the side of his temple, he added, "She had black hair, a little on the shorter side. Plump, never missed a meal." He smiled a bit from his own humor.

"So there were two women?" Glitch butted in.

"Sí. Other lady stayed in the car."

"Is that it?" Glitch asked while walking around the small store looking for clues.

"The plump señora has been here. Think she is staying with the recluse that lives across the river gorge. That's the word from the crop duster man down the street. He checks on the old recluse sometimes."

"How do we get to this man's house?" Javier asked.

The gas station man began to give them directions. Mentioning as many details as possible since it was very easy to get lost. They listened intently, Javier knowing in his gut that this was Maria and Esmeralda.

Glitch and Javier left the gas station confident in finding them both. He called Mateo to let him know where they were going, and to be prepared for his return the day after. Javier then spoke to Dr. Ruiz to consult with him on what to do about the medicine but just as they got into a detailed conversation, his phone cut off. Javier looked at his phone in disgust. There was no cell phone service out in the woods.

Javier wanted to think about the situation before confronting Esmeralda and I. He told Glitch to drive back to the last hotel they had seen so they could spend the night and get some sleep. He wanted this interaction to take place during the day because he was not familiar with the area, just in case it went bad.

They checked into the rundown, smelly hotel room and got settled. While lying in bed, Javier's mind was racing. He knew that these circumstances could possibly show itself. The medicine wasn't a guarantee. At this point, he was thinking about our lives as a married couple and not a business man. Could he win my affection without the use of medication? His heart was aching for me; really, for Maria.

Glitch, being half asleep, suddenly spoke, startling Javier. "So what's the plan Boss?"

Javier grumbled a bit. "I've been thinking. I'm pretty sure the women are Esmeralda and Maria." He said in an irritated tone, still thinking about me. "If we can find them, I'll probably have them taken to the island, to keep them isolated. Other than that, I have not made a decision yet."

"Do you think it is just the three of them in the house?"

"I'll call Mateo tomorrow to see if his hacker can get some satellite images before we go."

The next morning, Javier called Mateo using the land line in the hotel room, knowing it might be the last time he would communicate with his men.

"Hello." Mateo answered.

"Mateo I need you to contact Node and have him search the area that I am in." Javier continued to explain the location of the house. "Call this number back as soon as you can."

About an hour later, Mateo called with good news. He told Javier the layout of the land. That there were three heat signatures on the property and it was pretty isolated.

Pleased with the information, he felt confident that Glitch and himself could handle the encounter. They packed up their belongings in the room, got into the SUV and pulled away. Making their way through the roads encased with trees, the gravel popping up as they drove. It was much easier to navigate in the daylight. Reaching the questionable covered bridge crossing the river, Glitch and Javier discussed once more the plan they concocted for when they got to the house. Satisfied, Glitch drove forward.

When they reached the other end of the bridge, Javier saw the house that the old man had described.

"Pull over here Glitch." Javier said, while pointing to the side of the road.

Glitch parked the car along the shoulder of the road, hiding it from prying eyes. As they made their way up the dirt road, they pulled their guns out of their holsters. When they reached the house, they went in separate directions, patrolling around the perimeter trying to peer through each window, hoping to size up the situation before entering, with each man carefully inspecting their surroundings as they continued to walk.

Glitch had gone to the left, which was the shorter side of the house, walking past shrubs that needed trimming. As he made his way towards the back, he could hear people talking. Leaning against the corner of the house with his gun raised towards his chest, anticipating the confrontation, he first peeked around the corner to see what was going on.

Maximo, Esmeralda and myself were eating our lunch and discussing our plans to find Lucy. Just as we clinked our beer bottles together, Glitch came around the corner brandishing his gun. Startled by this unexpected visitor, Esmeralda and I stayed seated in our chairs but Maximo stood up, puffing his chest out as if he was a virile young man again, ready to protect us. Glitch slowly walked towards us, keeping his gun pointed in our direction while yelling out for Javier. Maximo, recognizing that we had the advantage, lunged at Glitch, knowing his fate to come. He screamed at us, "Run girls!"

Esmeralda immediately grabbed my hand, pulling me forward to follow her. Both of us running side by side as fast as we could towards the path into the woods. Bang!

Bang! I looked back just in time to see Maximo falling to the ground and Javier coming around the backside of the house looking at Glitch and Maximo. As the two of them convened on the patio, I faintly saw Glitch point at us. Communicating to Javier where we had gone.

As we got towards the end of the path by the river, Esmeralda stopped to catch her breath. Both of us were struggling, but Esmeralda was especially fighting for every puff of air.

"What should we do?" I implored as best as I could.

"We should separate. You head towards the bridge and I will distract them. The bridge is the easiest way out of here." Just as Esmeralda finished talking, we could hear twigs and sticks breaking under the feet of the two men.

We gave each other a quick hug and headed in opposite directions. Making my way towards the bridge, the dirt path became more and more narrow, causing me to slow down. The path transformed from soft dirt into mud, small boulders and thick foliage. It was becoming increasingly hard to navigate. Getting dangerously close to the edge of the cliff, anxiety was building up in my chest not only from the danger of falling, but knowing that Javier or Glitch was close behind.

It felt like I had been battling the terrain forever. I was tired, sweating and getting inflicted with pricks from thorns, taking each new step carefully, but willfully. I stopped for a quick look. I could barely see the bridge in the distance but it was there, giving me hope.

"Maria stop!" I turned my head out of astonishment.

Quickly and quietly, Javier caught up with me.

I didn't say anything. I scrambled as fast as I could, trying to move faster. The path finally started to open up again. I knew this was my opportunity to gain some ground on Javier. I glanced back at him to see him struggling but he was clearly stronger than me, he batted through the shrubbery fast. I could only take a few more steps before Javier fired his gun at me. He seemed to be aiming at the ground but it still made me stop in my tracks. I had nowhere to go, the forest was too thick and the gorge was twenty feet deep. As I whipped my head around to see what Javier was up to, he aimed in my direction again, firing. My instinct was to dodge the bullet, but it was a mistake. I stepped on an area of loose soil, falling backwards towards the river. Reaching my hands out to grab anything that would stop my fall. I tumbled a few feet, hitting tree branches, shrubs and protruding rocks, finally grasping a broken tree branch on my way down. The momentum of the fall forced my lower body to dangle below the branch, with only my two hands holding tight to the wooden protrusion as they bled from the impact.

"Maria! Are you okay?" Javier shouting in concern, still an air of love in his voice.

"Javier! Help!" I was struggling to hold on. My hands felt like they were on fire.

Javier finally reached my location. He leaned over the edge to see how far I had fallen. "Hold on. I'm gonna try to reach you." He strategically placed his hands and feet on anything that was stable, but it was too late.

"I can't hold on!"

"I'm almost there!" He yelled.

The roaring of the river below was calling my name. I started praying that there were no hidden rocks beneath the turbulent water. My hands started to lose their grip while Javier was struggling to get to me. It was just too difficult. I could feel the inevitable consequence arriving faster and faster. I could hold on no longer, my hands were free.

The rush of the frigid water engulfed my body and my senses. Holding my breath, trying to swim to the surface, the water swirled around my body as if it was grabbing me to keep me in its embrace. The churning rage holding me under and dragging me along the current eventually spat me out to where I could gasp for a breath of air. Kicking my feet and paddling with my hands, I was able to stable myself enough to see the shoreline. I was bobbing up and down helplessly while being dragged down river, almost reaching the covered bridge where the gorge was much shallower. The water was mercilessly splashing me in my face as I slammed into a protruding stump that was still partially tethered to the base of its tree. My hands were so cold that I could barely hold on but the fear of being pulled under the water again gave me the strength to pull myself ashore.

Lying on my back in the cold mud with my eyes closed, I enjoyed the warmth of the air penetrating my body. Knowing that I may not have much time, I sat up while feeling an excruciating pain in my right side. Wincing in agony, I managed to get to my feet, examining the hill that I had to ascend to get out of this mess. Luckily, this part of the riverbank was not very steep but it was still covered with trees and rocks.

"Ahhhh!" I screamed out loud. Something hit me in my back. A weakness engulfed my entire body. I looked around to see Glitch standing by the edge of the road, directly in front of the entrance to the covered bridge with a dart gun in his hand. My eyes couldn't focus anymore as I fell to my knees; everything went dark.

CHAPTER 16

"THE ISLAND"

"Maia! Maia wake up!" I felt someone pushing me on my left shoulder. I carefully moved from my side to my back. Looking around, trying to focus my eyes, Esmeralda came into view.

"Esmeralda? What happened?" I said as I looked around the room. "Where are we?"

"I don't know. Are you okay?"

"Yes, I think so." I said while lifting up my shirt to find a large bruise on my right side. "Are you?" I was concerned because I could see bruising on her arms and a small cut on her forehead.

Esmeralda touched the wound on her face. "I guess I didn't stand much of a chance. I can't believe they managed to catch us both. I'm sorry. I never should have got you involved."

"It was my choice. I told you that we are going to find Lucy and we will. We just need to get out of here."

I stood up and walked to the only door in the room, turning and pulling the knob to no avail. Out of frustration I leaned my forehead against the door and groaned. I heard Esmeralda moving in the room so I turned around to see her walking to one of the windows. She noticed that the sash lock was closed so she unlocked it and pulled up on the handle. We both stared at each other in amazement. The window actually opened! Just as she put one of her legs outside the window to straddle it, an alarm went off.

"Keep going!" I shouted. "I'm right behind you!" Thinking this could be our only chance to escape, I headed to the window. Esmeralda made her way outside, looking around, and keeping watch while I made my exit. As soon as I was fully outside, I heard someone unlocking the door, trying to get in.

"Run!" I screeched. We both took off with Esmeralda leading the way. We made our way past a swimming pool with perfectly manicured landscaping, tall palm trees and brilliant flowering plants.

"This way!" Esmeralda pointed to a dock with a Cabin Cruiser resting peacefully on the ice blue water. Moving as fast as we could down a brick pathway, thinking we would make it, out of nowhere, two men darted out of a pool house door, causing us to lose our lead.

Esmeralda was slowing down, her ailing body was being overworked. I could hear her breathing becoming lethargic. Stepping off the brick path onto the sandy beach only made things worse. Even I could feel the depth of the sand yielding easily. I tried to keep her moving but it was no use. We only got another couple of yards before the two men caught up with us.

"Stop! There is no escape from here!" Marco, one of the guards, said as he grabbed my arm. I immediately started hitting him, battling as hard as I could. The other man, Antonio, had ahold of Esmeralda but she had no fight in her. She was gasping for air as she held her hand to her chest. The man was actually being gentle with her, letting her recover on her own time.

"Calm down! Calm down Mrs. Alatorre!" Marco said, while still having a hold of me. Deciding the fight was useless at this point, I composed myself by fixing my hair, which was a disastrous mess from me flinging myself around, straightening out my shirt that was disheveled and standing up straight.

I asked the man, "Where are we? Is this Javier's doing?"

"Follow me and I will show you." He said as he let go of my arm and gestured towards the house.

Being free from his grip, I stepped towards Esmeralda to see if she was feeling better. Displaying a quick smile, indicating she was fine. We both headed towards the house. The man in front of us led the way while the other one walked behind.

The beach house was statuesque. A Caribbean style house painted yellow with a red clay roofing. The house had verandas covering each doorway, protecting the sliding doors that were completely made out of glass. Each space had its own living room style furniture on the patios.

We walked around to the side of the house where there was a small covered walkway that led to an arched doorway with steps. Making our way up the spiral staircase to the top, it opened up to a platform overlooking the property; round in shape, and fitted with a large telescope to see vast distances.

"Look around. This is an island ladies. There is nowhere to go." Marco, who directed us on our walk, pointed out.

We both examined our surroundings. I took note of everything I could see on the island. A sandy shoreline surrounded the entire island. It was mostly open land with scattered palm trees, flowering trees and a few singing birds. As I took in the mesmerizing view, I could see a helicopter pad and a boat dock. I admit, it was very beautiful to say the least. However, the focus wasn't the view; it was not a vacation, but a kidnap. To escape, the only way off the island that I could see was the boat.

Standing calmly, I closed my eyes taking in the warmth of the breeze on my face, the tranquility of the moment, wondering why all of this drama was happening to me. I felt defeated, helpless.

I could feel Esmeralda approaching me. She stood next to me without saying anything at first. She was giving me my space, to process the situation. Surprisingly, the two men were also waiting patiently.

"Maia. I'm never going to see Lucy again. I can feel it."

"I know what you mean. There is something about this place." I turned to the two men to ask the same question as before.

"Did my husband tell you to bring us here?"

"Yes, he did. We are to keep you here until he calls."

"Why?"

"You need to ask him that." The tall man gestured for us to follow him back down the staircase, "Let's go ladies." Esmeralda and I were taken to a new room attached to the pool house. It looked more like a hotel room. There were several beds, a bathroom, table and chairs and a small kitchenette.

Just as the man was going to close the door, he said, "We are going to bring you some food. Are you two hungry?"

Esmeralda's face lit up. "Yes! I am starving!"

"And something to drink." I butted in.

"Sure, by the way, don't waste your time trying to break out. This room and the attached room are completely locked down. I'm not chasing you again."

I plopped myself on one of the beds while Esmeralda looked around the room, opening cabinets, the refrigerator, and other closed doors. She finally came across the door that connected to another room. She opened it to look inside. Flipping on the light switch, she entered the room. Out of curiosity, I decided to follow her. We both inspected the room.

It had several stations with vanity mirrors sitting on top of tables and stools in front to sit on. It reminded me of my bathroom at home where I would put on makeup and fix my hair. I opened one of the drawers in the table to find different types of makeup; lipstick, eye shadow, eye liner, blush - everything a girl needs. On the side of the table, hanging by hooks, was a blow dryer, curling iron and flat iron.

"Nooooo! No, No!" Esmeralda cried.

"Esmeralda, what is it?"

"It's Lucy's jacket! She was here!" She fell to the floor, crying uncontrollably. I ran to her.

"Are you sure it's hers?"

"Yes! I am sure!" The jacket was definitely unique with all its sparkles and hand made graffiti.

This was a tragic revelation. An overwhelming sense of anger came over me. I knew I had a bad feeling about this place. The remoteness of the island, the security of the house and now this room. A room that was clearly used by women to doll themselves up, and make themselves pretty. Javier would bring the girls here, the ones he would traffic. I knew it.

I sat alongside Esmeralda, holding her as she cried her pain away. Consoling her was all I had to give. To console a mother who had come to the realization that she might never see her daughter again. I held her tight, stroked her hair to calm her down, hoping that I was making a difference.

After what seemed like forever, the room finally became quiet. I still kept a hold of her. She showed no signs of wanting to get up or even have a conversation. We sat in silence while she kept a tight hug around Lucy's jacket.

The room door made a creaking sound. It was being pushed open by Marco, the man who put us here. He entered the room halfway to find us on the floor between the makeup tables and a small couch.

"I put your food on the table in the other room. Eat before it gets cold." He spoke in an apathetic tone while leaving the door open behind him.

We didn't get up right away. It took Esmeralda a few minutes to compose herself. She wiped the tears away from her red, swollen eyes as she stood up. We never said a word to each other, just moved in unison. We both walked into the other room, sat down and ate. I looked at her many times to let her know that I was there to listen but she never looked away from her plate. She kept her head down the whole time, and was slowly eating with little whimpers in between bites.

A bright orange sun ray beamed through the window, turning my hand and dinner plate a brilliant hue. I looked over at the window to see a vibrant sunset hanging low in the sky. Pushing my chair away from the table, I got up to view its beauty. The sunsets were captivating from my house but this one was one of a kind. Yellow, orange, red and purple shades spread themselves throughout the sky. Little puffs of clouds, some translucent, floating around aimlessly without care. I leaned my body against the wall resting my head on the window casing, daydreaming. "How can the world be so majestic and cruel at the same time? How can someone say they love you, but hurt you willingly?" These thoughts lingered through my mind.

Esmeralda joined me. She leaned her warm body into mine. She wrapped one of her arms around my waist, staring out the window with me.

CHAPTER 17

"DISSATISFIED CLIENT"

Smoke swirled around in the air. A mix of cigarette and cigar smoke permeated the outbuilding on Javier's country property. Raul, Glitch and some of his other reliable men were loading their guns with ammunition. Dressed in all black, they looked like a group of mercenaries preparing for battle. Each man packed a bag with equipment and weapons in anticipation of a possible confrontation tonight.

Dust from the dirt floor rose slightly above the ground with every step the men took. Walking back and forth to the cars, they loaded each one as quickly as possible so that they could be ready when Javier would instruct them to roll out.

As soon as the men were throwing the last couple of bags into the cars, Javier was seen walking out of the front door of the log cabin. The main house sat atop a small grassy hill with large trees surrounding its perimeter, while the old, wooden outbuilding sat on the right side and slightly in front of the cabin. Connecting the two buildings was a dirt path just wide enough for vehicles.

As Javier approached, Glitch came out of the building to speak to him.

"What's the plan Boss?" Glitch asked while finishing his cigarette.

"We agreed to meet at El Clavadista tonight. Send a few of the boys now. I want them in place before Mr. Zhao and his men show up."

Glitch took one last drag off his cigarette, dropped it on the ground and smashed it with his foot. He started to turn to go inside when Javier had one more thing to say.

"Glitch. Tell Raul and Oscar to take the boat out and meet us there. To keep an eye out for us."

"Will do."

Walking inside to give instructions to the men who were going to leave first, he told them he wanted one guy to have Mr. Zhoa in his sight at all times and the other men were to surround the perimeter. Raul and Oscar were to watch from the boat, provide extra eyes for Javier and his men and also to watch out for the police.

El Clavadista was in the city which was popular with the locals and tourists during the day. It was a tower with a staircase that led to a platform at the top, meant for sightseeing. Some of the locals liked to cliff dive off the side of the tower where protruding rocks provided platforms, and provided entertainment for tourists. The meeting however was later in the night when there would be fewer people.

The day quickly and quietly transitioned into the night. Javier and his men left the country house for the city just as the sun was setting. They first drove on dirt roads of the rural towns, then to the paved roads outside the city, and onto the cobblestone streets throughout the historic districts in Mazatlán.

Javier gazed out the tinted window, watching the old city come alive with people, street vendors and drug dealers hanging out on the corners. Each black SUV followed the other in a straight line as if they were important government officials, while people kept staring at them as they went by, hoping to get a glimpse of those inside. The ocean finally made its appearance, indicating they were getting closer to their destination. Driving along the coastal road at a steady pace, a crumbling rock wall protected their cars and the city from crashing waves. Every minute or two, a wave could be heard crashing violently against large boulders, protruding from the ocean and the rock wall.

Javier's motorcade started to slow down. Arriving at the meeting point, they maintained some distance by parking along the road just before the walkway to El Clavadista. As the cars stopped, Javier's men jumped out of their respective cars to scan the surrounding area, with a few heading to the platform to make sure it was safe. The only men who stayed in the cars were the drivers. For the sake of appearances, Javier waited for Glitch to open his door before exiting. Putting one foot after the other on the ground, he stood erect with his chest puffed out, buttoning his suit jacket while looking to his left and right, purposefully projecting power.

There was no sign of Mr. Zhao and his men, so Javier made his way down the walkway, cautiously looking around. Just then Glitch's cell phone vibrated in his pocket. Answering it, he said, "Hello."

"Hey, it's Raul. No signs of movement out here." Raul and Oscar had been idling along the shoreline keeping watch. Sometimes, they used binoculars to see farther into the city.

"No movement here either." Glitch said. "Mr. Alatorre is heading to the platform."

"Understood." Raul confirmed.

Using his headset to speak to his snipper, Glitch checked in with him. "S1, are you in place?"

"S1 in place. Shot is clear."

"The Boss will scratch his temple for the go ahead shot."

"10-4."

One of the other men interrupted, "We've got movement. Two cars are parking behind ours."

"Confirmed." Another man agreed.

"Everyone stay alert. Remember we want to keep Mr. Zhao as a client but Mr. Alatorre will make the call." Glitch reiterated to his men. All the men checked in one by one, acknowledging the plan.

The group of Asian men made their way to Javier. Most of them looked young and inexperienced; but anyway, looks could be deceiving. However, Mr. Zhao was a middle aged, rotund man with medium length hair and a few moles strategically placed around his face. The larger one on his chin had a single black hair peeking out of the center, begging to be stared at.

Mr. Zhao was known for his eccentric personality, his lack of empathy and the brutal attacks on those who dared to betray him. If the meeting turned bad, it could cause a lot of problems for Javier's business. Javier had built his reputation on being a reliable source for pretty, and young girls, so the last set of girls that were released by Esmeralda put a stain on his reputation.

Two younger Asian men stepped onto the platform first, hands on guns but not drawn. Javier's men reacted by copying their movements. Everyone looked at each other with extreme caution. Within a few seconds, Mr. Zhao approached, signaling to his men to relax and calm down.

"Hello Mr. Zhao. I appreciate you taking this meeting." Javier said.

"How do you intend to make this right Mr. Alatorre? You have caused a disruption in my business network."

"I understand, but our relationship has been successful up to this point. I see no need to change things now. It's a small hiccup. My men and I are working hard on another shipment, better than the last one. You will be very happy."

"I see. That is good news, but how do I know this mistake won't happen again?"

"What are you requesting from me Mr. Zhao?"

"Punishment for the person who caused this. Clearly they are a threat."

Javier started to feel uncomfortable because he wasn't going to let Mr. Zhao know that it was his wife and housekeeper.

"The people responsible are being taken care of." Javier assured him.

"I want proof if you want to continue business with me. When you show me proof, then I will accept your new shipment and forget this ever happened." With that being said, Mr. Zhao signaled to his men that the meeting was over. He started to walk down the steps first, then his men followed behind watching Javier, Glitch and the others for any unexpected movements.

"What are you thinking Boss?" Glitch inquired softly under his breath.

Javier looked around for a second at this men, then put both of his hands in his pants pockets, made a grimace expression on his face and said, "Tell the men to head back to the country house."

Glitch contacted Raul on the boat, then his other men to rendezvous back at the house.

The car was quiet on the drive back. Glitch was driving but he frequently looked at Javier from the rear view mirror. The expressions on Javier's face indicated that his mind was working overtime. He was scheming up a master plan to get his relationship with Mr. Zhao back on track.

As they drove from the downtown area and into the suburbs, Javier asked Glitch to stop by his house. The Alatorre home was not close to their location but Javier needed some time alone in a different environment. He missed me. He missed his home life with me.

About thirty minutes later, Glitch pulled the SUV in front of our house. The house was beautiful at night. The driveway had solar lights illuminating its path. Small accent lights lit up some of the sculptured bushes on the grounds. Most of the house was constructed of glass to take advantage of the views, but a few brick accent walls were placed throughout, with each one having a flood light accentuating its beauty and stony roughness. However, the inside was eerily dark and empty; devoid of any life.

"I'll wait for you here Mr. Alatorre." Glitch put the car in park.

"I changed my mind. I think I will stay here for the night. Come back and pick me up in the morning." Javier opened the back door to get out.

Glitch rolled down his window. When Javier came around to his side of the car by the sidewalk leading to his home, Glitch turned his head towards the window opening and said, "All right. If you need anything just call me."

"I'll be fine."

Glitch rolled up his window as he drove away. Javier used the keypad on the door to get inside. Walking through the house in the dark, he made his way into his office. Turning on a light was unnecessary, the full moon was shining brightly through the windows, illuminating everything it touched.

He maneuvered his way to the small bar in the corner of the room and made himself a glass of Whiskey. Walking towards the wall of windows, he opened one of the slider doors to let the ocean breeze inside. Standing at the door opening, looking out at the white ocean caps being highlighted by the moon, he took a swig of his drink.

Even though it was late, Javier decided to call the beach house to check on us. The phone rang a couple of times before one of his men answered.

"Hello?" Marco answered.

"I'm just checking on the girls. How's it going there?"

"We had an incident. They got out of the house but everything is fine now. We took them to the lookout. I think they understand their situation now."

"Good. How is Maria?"

"I think she is more worried about Esmeralda than herself. But she is fine Mr. Alatorre."

"I'll check back in tomorrow." Javier hung up the phone.

The feeling of missing me was taking a toll on Javier. He never really grieved for his real wife. It wasn't long after her death that he found out about me. Then things moved very quickly.

Javier went to his desk and turned on his laptop. Sitting down in his chair, he took another drink of his Whiskey while waiting for his computer to boot up. After logging in, he opened a secret file hidden within other folders. They were old photos; not of me, but of the real Maria. He scrolled through old photographs of her. The light from the laptop was flashing on Javier's face, changing with each mouse click. Javier started to contemplate the fact that the real Maria was gone forever; that he may never be able to talk me into staying.

CHAPTER 18

"FAREWELL"

The sunshine failed to show up this morning. The sky was gloomy, exhibiting all signs that rain was on its way. I noticed that Esmeralda was still sleeping. Being as quiet as possible, I walked over to take a glance at her to make sure she was okay. The bed covers enveloped her lower body but her upper body was uncovered, exposing her arms wrapped around Lucy's jacket. Her face was puffy and slightly red, probably from crying for the most of the night.

I went into the bathroom to freshen myself up. Standing, looking at myself in the mirror, I started to wonder what was going to happen to us. We couldn't be held captive forever. Esmeralda and I needed to figure a way out of this mess. We needed to take some chances.

Our lives changed so quickly. It felt like it was just the other day I woke up from my coma; Esmeralda was cooking me breakfast every day and Javier was acting like a loving husband. Yet, my reality changed in a snap of a finger; I was in some strange house, on a remote island with strange men watching my every move.

An overwhelming feeling came over my body. My hands started to shake a little, my heart felt like it was racing. I felt hot and sweaty. Turning on the cold water, I leaned over the sink to splash some water on my face. I felt nauseous so I stayed bent over the sink, putting both my elbows on the counter on either side of the sink bowl to keep me stable while wrapping my arms around the sink as if I was giving it a hug. A light knock on the door startled me.

"Maia? Are you okay?" Esmeralda said through the closed door.

"Yeah, I'm fine. I'll be out in a minute."

I splashed more water on my face and turned off the faucet. I let the water penetrate my skin for a few seconds; the cooling effect helped me feel better. I dabbed my face with a towel until it was dry, fixed my hair where it got wet and opened the door to see if Esmeralda needed me.

She was sitting quietly on the edge of the bed mumbling to herself. She seemed off, as if she was in a daze. I slowly strolled over to her, and sat next to her on the bed.

"Hey! Why don't we ask if we can take a walk on the beach before it rains?" She did not respond.

"Esmeralda?" I gently rubbed the top of her leg to try to get her attention. "Do you want to take a walk on the beach? Get some fresh air?"

She covered my hand with one of hers, and shook her head in approval.

"Let me see what I can do."

I walked over to the door and started banging as loud as I could, saying hello to anyone that could hear me. It didn't take long before Antonio opened the door. "What can I do for you Mrs. Alatorre?"

"We're not doing so good cooped up in here. We want to take a walk on the beach and get some fresh air."

"It's going to rain." He remarked in a deep voice.

"It's not raining yet. Look how far away those clouds are." I pointed towards the window.

He appeared sympathetic. He didn't look like a typical henchman. He was on the younger side, good looking for what it's worth, with no visible battle scars like the other men. He pulled a two-way radio off the side of his belt, pressed a button and spoke to someone on the other end.

"Be alert. I am taking Mrs. Alatorre and Ms. Garcia out for a walk. I need someone to meet us by the boat dock."

"Maybe we can eat our breakfast outside too?" I quickly added.

"They would like to eat breakfast by the pool. Set it up there." Dropping the radio down by his side he said sarcastically, "Will that be all?"

"Yes. Thank you. I appreciate you being so nice."

"We'll go when you two are ready."

"We're ready now!" I said enthusiastically.

Esmeralda must have been paying attention because she got up on her own and headed to the door to meet up with us. Smiling at her I grabbed her hand, both of us following the young man outside.

When we reached the sand, Javier's men backed off so we could be alone. The breeze on our faces felt wonderful. We slowly strolled along the beach absorbing every moment, and all the beauty the island offered. Esmeralda started to perk up with every stride; she was looking down, examining all the seashells, picking up one or two to take back to the room. It felt so freeing to feel the sand between my toes. The water crashing along the shoreline and then floated its way up to my feet. My foot prints left their mark and then disappeared with the next rush of salt water.

Eventually, we passed the boat dock which was housing the only motorized escape from the island. The Cabin Cruiser bobbed up and down with every wave that rolled in. I couldn't help but fantasize about jumping into it, magically finding the keys already in the ignition, and driving off. As we drove away, with Esmeralda and I turning our heads to watch the island get smaller and smaller, the men desperately running to the edge of the dock to stop us. My fantasy didn't last long; Esmeralda woke me up when she placed her arm across the front of my body to prevent me from stepping onto a bunch of sticks, branches and other debris along the beach. It looked like we had to turn around and head back. It was for the best. When we turned around, I looked towards the house and I could see our food being placed at the table by the pool. We headed back to the house but maintained our same walking path to take advantage of our freedom while we had it, making it last as long as possible.

By the time we got to the table, our food was lukewarm. However it was worth it. Javier's men continued to keep a close eye on use as we ate. For the most part, Esmeralda and I sat in silence, chit chatting every so often. To be honest, there wasn't much to say, at least not in front of Javier's men.

While sipping on a cup of coffee, I noticed Marco talking on his cell phone, occasionally looking back at us. He raised his hand, and used a finger to call over Ricardo. A heavier set middle aged man who was almost bald, was standing about fifty feet away by the archway leading to the lookout tower. He happily complied with the request. As soon as he reached Marco, he stopped and waited for instructions.

"When do you need this done Mr. Alatorre?"

"As soon as possible."

"I'll call you when it's done." Both men hung up the phone.

Javie's men started to gather in a group, talking amongst themselves. I watched them closely, wondering what was happening. Antonio and Ricardo walked off towards the boat dock while Marco came over to us.

"Ladies, that was Mr. Alatorre on the phone. I told him how much you were enjoying your outside walk so he suggested taking you on a boat ride before it rains."

"I think we are good here." I remarked nervously.

"I want to go!" Esmeralda chimed in.

"Esmeralda I don't think it is a good idea. Look at the sky." I pointed to the dark clouds.

"We can just go around the island. It won't take long." Esmeralda tried to make a point.

"Yes Mrs. Alatorre, it won't take long. We'll keep an eye out for any weather changes." He said in a softer voice, trying to sound friendly. He leaned in towards me, pulling my chair out, and forcing me to stand up. Esmeralda saw this and followed suit. I thought to myself, *"She is not thinking clearly."*

Pulling on my arm to get me moving, he escorted me to the boat while Esmeralda followed happily behind. Antonio was standing on the dock waiting for us to board so he could untie the boat. The boat was already running and ready to sail. Esmeralda and I were guided to the spot where we were told to sit. Antonio jumped on board and as soon as our bottoms hit the cushions, Marco drove the boat slowly away from the dock.

We made our way around the island; this did not take long. I assumed we were going to go back to the dock but we didn't end up doing that. The boat turned towards the open ocean. I looked at the horizon; it was dark with billowing clouds growing larger and larger as they moved our way. I looked over my shoulder, the taller palm trees on the island began to sway back and forth from the gusts of wind swirling around the island. The storm was almost here.

"Where are we going?" I asked. Nobody answered me. They continued to drive farther and farther out. Fifteen minutes had passed. I felt little raindrops hitting my face. "We are not going to make it back before the storm hits." I thought to myself. On the spur of the moment, I exclaimed;

"We need to turn around! What is wrong with you! Turn around!" My shouting fell on deaf ears.

All of a sudden, the boat slowed down to a stop. We were idling in the water at the mercy of the waves. Up and down, up and down we went. The rain started coming down even harder. I noticed a red buoy floating in the water. Ricardo reached out over the boat for something. I tried to look around his body but just as I did, Antonio took Esmeralda and dragged her towards the front of the boat.

"What's going on? " Hollering as loudly as I could. "What are you doing! Let her go!"

I began grabbing and kicking Antonio. I told Esmeralda to fight back. She did not. Her eyes swelled with tears. She was at ease.

Marco let go of the wheel and reached his arms around my entire body, pulling me away from the confrontation. I tried desperately to stop what was happening, doing whatever it took to stop them from hurting my only friend.

It was a rope. Ricardo had a rope in his hand and he started to wrap it around Esmeralda's feet while Antonio tied her wrists. Esmeralda stood silent. She did not fight. She knew her fate.

"Maia stop." She said in an eerily calm voice. "I knew this day would come. They won't hurt you. Javier would never let them hurt you."

"No! Don't give up! I need you!" I was still trying to get out of the man's grip.

"I need you to tell Javier something for me. Will you promise to tell him?"

"Yes! Yes!"

"Lucy is Javier's daughter." She lowered her head in shame.

"What?" I stopped in my tracks, stunned.

"Javier and I had an affair. I kept it a secret because I didn't want her to be dragged into his lifestyle or his business." She looked directly into my eyes at that moment. "He needs to get her back!"

"Esmeralda!" I screamed as I watched them throw her overboard. Ricardo videotaped the whole thing with a straight face, as if he had no conscience. I saw Esmeralda try to keep her head above the water, desperately gasping for air. Going under the water, popping back up when she had enough strength to kick her legs, and disappearing after a couple of attempts. She was gone!

My blind rage kicked in. Screaming, propelling myself forward to the spot where she went over, I impulsively went after Ricardo for videotaping it, knocking it out of his hand causing it to go overboard. The camera immediately started to sink down below the water. I looked over the side of the boat looking for any sign of her. Nothing! Nothing!

I was grabbed from behind and thrown backwards into the arms of Marco. The other two men were arguing with each other over the lost video camera. They were accusing each other of not being responsible and bickered over who was going to tell Mr. Alatorre.

Nobody spoke a word on the ride back. I sat back down in my seat whimpering and trying to protect myself from the pounding rain. Marco was attempting to keep the boat from capsizing due to the high waves that developed. The storm was raging. "Maybe we would all be lost!" I feared.

CHAPTER 19

"PAYING THE PRICE"

The next morning was a solemn one. I laid in bed for the most of the morning under the covers. Eyes closed, brain shut down, depressed for the most part. My so-called husband was a criminal, my friends were merely Javier's thugs. I had no real family that I knew of and my only friend was dead. My life did not seem real.

I just started to doze off again when the bedroom door opened. The squeaking noise peaked my curiosity. I moved the covers off my head just enough for my eyes to see who was in the room. It was Marco.

"Mrs. Alatorre?" He said loudly, not holding back. "Mr. Alatorre is on his way to see you."

"So what? I don't want to see him." I put the covers back over my eyes.

"Get up and get dressed." He walked out without waiting for a response from me.

I rolled over on my back, uncovered the top half of my body and stared at the ceiling. Once again, I was being bossed around by another person. I rolled my eyes and reluctantly dragged myself out of bed. I took my time getting ready, while walking around like a sloth; sitting on the bed every once in a while gazing out the window.

The sky was a pretty shade of blue that day. Maybe the storm washed away the air pollution. It seemed crisp and clear until a loud helicopter appeared out of nowhere. I walked over to the window to see what was going on.

I saw Javier jump out of the helicopter, walking quickly until he cleared the blades whipping by his head. I immediately noticed how handsome he was. He wasn't dressed in a suit this time. A coral colored Polo shirt, white jeans and white boat shoes. He grew a goatee beard which made him look even more dapper. My heart fluttered a little bit.

Antonio and Ricardo waited by the pool, looking at their watches and adjusting their white shirt collars, trying to act professional in front of their boss. Javier finally made his way from the perfectly manicured grass to the stone sidewalk leading to his men. Greeting them with a smile, Javier shook their hands. He appeared to be in a good mood. I eventually lost sight of them when they walked inside.

They all gathered in a room decorated with sports memorabilia. A leather sectional couch facing a large big screen TV that hung on the wall and a wet bar on the opposite side of the room. Marco was behind the bar, having already poured glasses of Whiskey and laid out Cuban cigars on the counter. The first thing Javier did was take a huge swig of the Whiskey, looked at the glass with a satisfying smirk, then put it back down on the bar counter where it was quickly refilled. The other men followed suit waiting for their Boss to speak first.

"How's Maria doing?" Javier took another drink.

"Not good. She has shut down." Antonio said as he sat on a bar stool a couple of stools away.

"She needed to see that." Javier said.

"We do have a problem though." Marco tried to initiate a conversation that was going to be hard to discuss.

"What's that?" Javier asked. All the men looked at each other waiting for someone to tell him the bad news about the camera.

Ricardo, who dropped the camera, stepped forward to tell his Boss his mistake. "The video camera was knocked out of my hand and into the water. I'm sorry Boss. It sank fast."

The anger on Javier's face was very noticeable. He took another drink but this time he slammed the glass on the table, breaking it.

"Do you know what this means?" Javier asked.

All the men looked at each other again unsure of how to respond. Marco quickly got Javier a new glass.

"Huh? Do you know what this is going to cost me! How hard is it to get rid of an inferior female?"

Ricardo answered. "Mrs. Alatorre went crazy. I wasn't prepared for that. It was my fault."

Javier walked over to him. Ricardo was standing a few steps from the bar in between Javier and Antonio. Javier looked him in the eye, took his right hand and placed it behind his neck pulling his head forward so Javier could get into this face.

"Mr. Zhao is expecting proof! This may cost me millions of dollars! Money I need to pay you, my other men and to run my business! Not to mention my reputation!"

"I'm sorry Boss. I'm sorry. I'll do whatever you need to make it right."

Javier let go of Ricardo while at the same time pushing him a little backwards with his other hand. He stumbled a bit but remained on his feet. Javier returned to his post at the bar, bent over leaning on his two elbows, thinking. Picking up his glass, he swirled it around, watching the ice cube and alcohol move together in unison. After a minute or two, Javier told Marco, who was still behind the bar, to stay with him and told the other two men to leave.

As soon as they cleared the room, Javier conveyed a new plan to save his business. A plan they would execute immediately because time was running out. Mr. Zhao had contacted Javier late last night, telling him that he needed a new shipment soon so he wanted proof right away if they wanted to continue business together.

"Now that we have a game plan, we can talk about the plans with my wife tonight."

"Did you get the Chef you wanted?" Marco asked.

"Yes, everyone has a price." Javier took another drink, standing up tall. "The helicopter will bring him and two other cooks back here about 5. They're going to set up a table out on the beach. Bring Maria around 6:30. I plan on meeting her there."

"You don't want to see her before that?"

"I want to give her time to cool off. I also need to cool off."

Marco walked from behind the bar telling Javier, "Okay. I will go let her know she has a date."

He exited the room and left Javier alone. Javier finished his drink, then headed outside to meet up with his other men. While Javier was having a casual conversation with them, Marco talked to me.

"Mrs. Alatorre?" He knocked a few times quickly.

I opened the door. "What's going on?" Rolling my eyes at him. "I see Javier is here."

"Mr. Alatorre wants you to join him tonight for dinner."

"I don't want to see him."

"I don't think you have a choice. I will be back at 6:30 to get you. I'm pretty sure you can find a nice dress to fit you in the closet."

"You mean where the girls that you kidnap stay."

"I'll be back later." He shut the door and headed back to Javier.

All of Javier's men gathered outside. At first, they stood in a semi-circle conversing, but it rapidly turned into Javier telling his men to follow him. They walked past the swimming pool, the pool house and onto the stone pathway towards the helicopter pad. As they were walking, Javier told his plan to the others.

"Antonio is going to stay here and help me. Marco, I want you and Ricardo to help the pilot go pick up the chefs and bring them back here."

"Yes Sir." Marco and Ricardo said in almost complete unison.

Javier and Antonio stood by the helicopter while the pilot started it up. The blades started swirling around, picking up speed as Marco and Ricardo boarded, leaving the doors open as they took off.

The three men flew away, disappearing in the blue sky, making their way back to the mainland. About thirty minutes into the flight, Marco tapped the pilot on his shoulder. In response, he started to drift the helicopter a little lower towards the open ocean. When he got to the altitude he wanted, he leveled the helicopter and used his right hand to hold his cell phone towards the back seat and pressed record. Ricardo took notice.

"What's going on?"

Marco didn't answer. He looked at the camera to confirm it was recording, pulled out his gun and shot Ricardo three times. Ricardo grabbed his chest where he was shot. Blood started to ooze out from behind Ricardo's hands. Leaning his head back against the seat, he started to make a wheezing sound as he took each breath.

"Mr. Zhao will be satisfied."

"That's the plan."

Marco didn't flinch once. He put his gun back into its holster, took the phone from the pilot's hand to finish recording Ricardo being pushed out the open door. Marco made sure to videotape until he hit the water; a successful kill.

CHAPTER 20

I stood in front of the window in my room watching the clock. The sun was getting low in the sky, producing beautiful red and orange colors, with thin, purple clouds spreading out at the horizon, never disappointing the eyes.

I had a sick feeling in the pit of my stomach. I was torn. I wanted to see Javier to confront him but at the same time I never wanted to see his face again. I was feeling confused and a little disoriented. I told myself I had to remember who he really is, what he did to Esmeralda, Lucy and myself.

I walked around the room nervously in my red dress. The closet did have a large collection of clothes but most of them were too revealing. Modesty was best for this situation. I wanted him to see me as Maia, not Maria.

I looked at the clock. It was time. I was facing the opposite direction, so I turned towards the room's door expecting one of Javier's men to open it at any moment. No knock on the door yet. Just as I turned around to pace back in the other direction, I heard it. Knock. Knock.

"Mrs. Alatorre I'm coming in." It was the younger man, Antonio. He opened to door and entered the room.

"Mr. Alatorre is ready for you."

I couldn't move at first, standing there wringing my hands around each other. I just stared at him, noticing how young he really was and wondered how he became involved with Javier.

"Mrs. Alatorre, are you ready?"

"I suppose." I said reluctantly as I walked in his direction and then out the door, with him following behind. I quickly realized I did not know this house. "Where are we going?"

"Follow me." He said.

I let him pass to lead the way. We walked through several hallways. I never got to see the larger rooms. I noticed the walls were bare, very plain. The path we took did not feel like a home, it felt like a hotel corridor without the gaudy carpet and not as many rooms.

He led me outside the house, onto a part of the property that I had not seen yet. The walkway was the same stone by the pool, lined with flowering plants that filled the air with their scent and tall skinny palm trees scattered throughout the grounds. I looked ahead to see lit tiki torches on the beach and a table set for two. I did not see Javier though. There was a female in a white chef's outfit, standing next to a smaller table.

"Here we are Mrs. Alatorre." He stopped to let me catch up and pointed his hand towards to table, gesturing for me to have a seat. I took his offer and walked over towards the table to sit down but not before he pulled out the chair to help me. We were in the sand so it was not easy to move the chair. The lady serving the drinks trudged her way to me, said hello, and poured a glass of white wine in both of our glasses. Out of the corner of my eye, I noticed Javier making his way to me. He changed his clothes to a light grey cotton suit with a white shirt. He left the top two buttons open, exposing his chest hair. I kept telling myself, "*He's not sexy. He's a bad man. A bad man!*"

"Hello my delicate flower." He leaned in to give me a kiss on the top of my head. It's usually on my cheek. But this time, I was grateful. He sat down in his chair looking at me as if he was trying to read my mind. I could feel the tension between us. I wanted to tell him to never call me that again. I knew why he called me that. That was the name of the boat my real husband and I were on when Javier sent his men to buy me. I held back though. I waited to see what else he had to say.

"Have my men been treating you well?" He asked as he picked up his glass of wine to take a drink.

"Yes, but I cannot say the same for Esmeralda." I responded sarcastically to see if he had anything to say. It didn't affect him. It rolled right off his back.

"You look beautiful." Trying to give compliments in hope that I would forgive and forget.

I did not respond. His compliments made me very uncomfortable. So uncomfortable that I could barely look at him. Luckily, the other two Chefs made their way to our table, putting our meal down in front of us at the same time.

"Enjoy your meal Mr. and Mrs. Alatorre." The head Chef then signaled for the others to follow him so we could be alone.

"Wow. It smells delicious!" He started eating, acting as if things were normal, like nothing had happened.

I couldn't decide what to do so I started eating too, watching him closely. He occasionally looked at me, raising his eyebrows as if he was waiting for a question from me but I never said anything. I was making a plan in my head on how to confront him but the truth is that there was only one way, and that was to just blurt out my feelings.

"Why did my real husband sell me to you?" I said with a lump in my throat.

"What are you talking about?"

"I know the truth." I quickly responded, then took a sip of my wine hoping it would provide me with some strength. "Esmeralda told me everything and now that I am not taking those fake pills you and Dr. Ruiz gave me, my memory is quite clear."

Javier leaned back into his seat. His facial expressions changed quickly. "You are confused right now. Let's finish eating this nice meal and then we can talk."

"I'm not confused. You're acting as if the last couple of days never happened." I started to get very upset. I took the white cloth napkin from my lap and threw it on the table.

"Delicate Flower, that is the name of my real husband's yacht. I remember seeing it when your men drove me away on their boat. But the fact that you call me that as a term of endearment is sick!"

"Maria, you are not quite yourself tonight. Why are you acting like this?" Javier perked up quickly, realizing his plan of action seemed not to be working.

"What! What is wrong with you! This tactic is not going to work on me. I see you for who you are. A bad, dangerous man who sells women for profit. Innocent young girls! I helped Esmeralda free the ones in the basement cells. I helped! Is that why you had her killed? You thought it was just her?"

"Maria, please calm down. You are ruining our evening." He reached out over the table to try and touch my hand but I wanted nothing to do with him. I reacted impulsively.

"My name is not Maria! It's Maia!" I got up from the table and stormed off, screaming and walking as fast as I could through the thick sand. I could not take being called that name anymore. I knew the truth and he was not going to persuade me otherwise.

I turned around to see what Javier was up to. He took off his jacket and jogged towards me. Never slowing down, I kept walking. It was dark outside so only the moonlight was lighting my walking path on the beach.

"Maria!" Javier grabbed my arm and spun me around into his chest. Holding me tight so I could not run away again. His body felt so warm. It was nice to be hugged by him again. Things felt normal for a split second.

"I told you my name is Maia!" I started to cry while looking into his eyes for some compassion.

"I need you in my life. We can get past this."

Both of my arms were pushed up against his chest. I tried to push away but he was too strong. I kept wiggling, hoping to loosen his bear hug. I was not going to give into him. I was not going to let him manipulate me.

"Forgive you! I will never forgive you for ruining my life, not to mention killing my only friend and trafficking your own daughter!"

All of the sudden I felt Javier's grip loosen. He slowly let me go. He took a step backwards, looking at me while rubbing his hand over his goatee several times. Placing his left hand into his pants pocket.

"What did you say?" He seemed very uneasy at that moment.

"Lucy. She is your daughter. You sold your daughter."

"Who told you this?"

"Esmeralda. Right before your men threw her overboard. She said you had an affair and that Lucy was your daughter."

"Oh my God."

"She wants you to get her back. That was her last wish."

"Why didn't she tell me!"

"Why? Look at your life. She wanted nothing to do with you. She protected her from you!"

"Shut up! Just shut up!" Javier got very angry, pointing his finger at me as if to dominate me. "If I knew, I would have taken care of both of them. I could have protected them!"

"You need to find a way to get her back." I said in a soft voice, trying to calm down the situation. "And you need to let me go."

Javier turned around and started walking back to the house. He never said another word to me.

He needed some privacy so he went to the lookout tower. Step by step, he climbed to the top of the platform, looking out at the vast ocean wondering how he could fix this huge mistake. Javier was a very prideful man but this time, this time he needed to swallow that pride for the sake of his daughter. He took his cell phone out of his pocket and dialed the phone.

"Hello. Mr. Sato, this is Mr. Alatorre."

"This is an early phone call."

"I know but I need to ask a huge favor. One that I will be indebted to you forever."

"I'm listening." He said inquisitively.

"The young girl you won at my auction. I would like to make a trade."

"I don't know if I can do that Mr. Alatorre. I am very fond of her."

"I understand but I have someone I think you would be very happy with. Just as beautiful but more experienced. Can I send you a picture?"

"Go ahead."

Javier sent a picture though a text to Mr. Sato. He was very impressed. He wondered how Javier always had access to such beautiful women.

"Mr. Alatorre, who is she?" Mr. Sato inquired.

"Her name is Maia. I'm offering her to you first."

"She is acceptable but she is not as young as Lucy. I will get much more use out of Lucy."

"What about adding some money to the deal?" Javier was not going to give up. He was very persuasive and knew Mr. Sato loved to make deals. Making a grumbling sound at first, then finally answering.

"The trade and $250,000. That's my offer."

"Sold!"